SREPSKA

A NOVEL BY
LUCAS STERLING

Nurrebul Productions, help@nurrebbulproductions.com

ISBN 978-0-9993387-0-4 978-0-9993387-1-1 (ebook)

First Edition

CHAPTER 1

Nairobi, Kenya

JULIUS OMENDA HAD no idea that the city had already fallen. He put on his good blue shirt, along with his tan pants. He'd gotten a stain yesterday, down on the back side of one leg when a clumsy British woman dropped his coffee. He'd scrubbed and scrubbed it, but it wouldn't come out. At least it wasn't too noticeable now.

As he combed his hair in the hall bathroom mirror, he thought back to what he watched on television last night. This panic about everybody's money worried him. His family back home depended on his wages and tips.

In the kitchen, the coffee cups and dishes from the day before were still piled in the sink. His roommate, who left earlier than he did, hadn't made coffee. Perhaps because he never came home last night. He probably was asked to work another shift in the kitchen at the Hotel Intercontinental.

Julius glanced down at his phone. He was expecting a confirmation text from the two groups that he was scheduled to pick up at the downtown Hilton. But there were no new messages. Even though he knew he hadn't missed anything, he checked the text messages in his archive. In passing, he glanced at the text message from several days earlier from the man who had lent him money to purchase his white Hi-Ace Toyota eight-seater van. It was yet another reminder that without a payment he would lose his van. The one he needed to drive tourists around.

As he jumped up into his van, his cellphone flashed the message: "searching for network connection." He angrily tossed the phone into the console, cursing under his breath. He glanced at the picture of his wife and young daughter taped on the dashboard. He cranked down the window to let in some air. Why did everything have to go wrong all at the same time?

His nose wrinkled, and he wondered what was causing the nauseating smell. Miles off, he saw smoke rising from large portions of downtown. What in the world was going on?

As he drove toward the highway, he noticed a lot more traffic than usual. Practically every car had several people crammed into it. The drivers of mopeds designed to carry only one person were carrying a passenger behind.

He made the decision to suddenly turn onto a minor road. It would likely be a faster route to the hotel. But that road wasn't much better—and then he reached a point where the traffic was hopelessly stopped. He couldn't go any farther. Like many others, he put his car in park and stood from the door to find out what was happening ahead. He felt a spark of fear as he spotted a crowd of men using wooden planks and pipes to smash windows and overturn cars up ahead. The smoke, he realized, must be coming from burning cars.

He covered his face with a cloth to help muffle the repulsive smell. Nearly all of the dozen cars that were on fire were government vehicles except for a late-model Lexus SUV. He reflectively buckled his knees to take cover the first time that he heard, over the shouts of the crowd, glass from a window break and hit the concrete. Then it happened again. And yet again.

"What is happening?" he asked a man driving an old car in a hotel uniform.

"I just need to get to my job," the stranger replied.

"I can't reach my family. The phones aren't working. I need to get to work today so I can afford to go home and see them. And I think this is the last tour I am giving. We are going to find a way to make ends meet where we can all live together, you know."

The stranger's face didn't change. Everybody had their own problems.

The traffic wasn't moving. Minutes turned into what felt like hours. Enough cars behind him—and ahead of him—had been abandoned that turning around was no longer an option.

He eventually pulled his van off into a parking lot that had more vehicles than parking spaces. He had to park more on the sidewalk than in the lot, but the thought of getting a parking ticket never crossed his mind. Every lane within eyesight was blocked with cars. As he locked the doors, he noticed several others sitting on the hoods or bumpers of their vehicles, smoking cigarettes.

He came upon a little cart with an umbrella over it. A teenager wearing a faded New York Mets t-shirt and khaki shorts was handing over a small cup of mixed fresh passion fruit and pineapples to a customer, accepting a couple bills in exchange. He went up to the stand and chatted up the seller. "You must be busy with all these people," he quipped as he pointed to a coconut. He reached into his pocket and pulled out a dollar. "Be thankful. My business is slower than ever these days."

"It will get better, man," the seller said, disinterested.

Julius kept walking, remembering that the promise of the next big series of groups kept him going. *They* always came, the tours that resulted in him hiring others to help. But when *they* came was difficult to predict. He had to be patient during the slow weeks as he waited for a phone call or email inquiring about his availability to conduct a tour.

Julius soon joined a group of people walking toward the city center. This was also where the Hilton was located. As he got closer, the crowd grew louder and bolder. Yet he was pleased to realize that he wasn't the only passive bystander. Despite what the crazy activity would suggest, only a small minority was instigating the chaos. Everyone else was trying to ignore them.

Julius took out his phone and recorded video of all that was happening. He could not readily tell who was leading the riot, if anyone was.

He followed the crowds, heading in a westerly direction. Soon he reached the State House, the traditional home of the president of Kenya. He didn't have a good view, but he could hear people shaking the gates in front of the presidential residence. Soon, the loud clangs of metal pipes being swung against the metal gate eclipsed the chanting of the crowds.

A television in a window of a coffee shop that amazingly was unscathed was playing CNN. He poked his head up to the window and saw that the news was covering what was happening in Kenya. "In Kenya, from farmers being paid for crops to ordinary citizens paying everyday expenses, the cellphone is the tool of choice. Many farmers and workers are paid via a transfer of money to their phone, which is in turn used to pay everyday bills. For Kenyans, the cellphone is basically their bank account, as only about ten percent of the population have a traditional checking or savings account. The Central Bank estimates that around forty percent of the nation's monthly gross domestic product is transferred using cellphones. Cellphones have largely replaced cash as the medium of payment for everyday people in this African nation," the anchor said.

The TV showed footage of people banging on the doors to get into the governmental complex downtown, some distance away from where he was. The footage showed how some people had begun attacking the iron bars around the windows with sledgehammers.

"The throngs in the streets are becoming angrier, louder, and harder to control. A fire is burning in a large bank building across from the governmental complex. The headquarters for the phone company is also on fire. Fire trucks cannot get to the buildings because the throngs of people are keeping the fire trucks a safe distance away."

"We are seeing what happens when cellphones, which happens to be where a sizable percentage of the population keeps their money, suddenly doesn't work. Stay tuned as this story continues to develop."

Julius took his eyes off the television as he heard loud arguing at the check-out counter. From the back and forth, he realized that the neatly dressed person seeking to make the transaction needed food for an elderly diabetic mother, yet he had no cash. And, his credit card could not be processed to pay for the transaction.

Julius turned around and headed out. As he did, a young man stuck a sign in his hands. "March with us to take back your country."

Julius dropped the sign instantly. "I want no part of this," he said. "This is insane. I cannot work, I cannot earn money. This is all crazy talk."

The man yelled to his compatriots, "We have a government plant here. He doesn't want us to succeed. He wants us to be taken advantage of…"

"Take the sign!" another man said.

Julius repeated what he said earlier. "How am I supposed to take care of my family with all this?" he shouted as he pointed his finger in the man's face.

Another in the group quickly approached Julius from behind as he was arguing and swung a two-by-four at his head. One swing was followed by several more swings, even after Julius had crumpled to the ground, helpless.

The marching and shouting went on, all captured on cameras from an independent tele-journalist who would soon sell the footage to BBC. "A man has been savagely beaten for merely not going along with the protesters. It is too early to determine if he is dead or alive."

Srepska had claimed another victim.

CHAPTER 2

OVER FIVE THOUSAND miles away from the erupting chaos in Kenya, Fredric Ulrich maneuvered his white carbon-fiber road bike through the traffic in Munich. To his left cars whizzed by him, some so close that he could feel being pulled toward them. With all the maniacs on this autobahn, he didn't want to end up as road kill.

The GPS unit on his bike showed that he had finished his sixty minutes. Fredric, wearing a thick yellow long-sleeve vest and compression bike pants, had covered the equivalent of twenty-two miles on this ride. That was the kind of fast pace he liked. There was no snow, although the splotches of sand and salt on the pavement were testament to recent snow that had since melted. Braving the cold for a midday workout gave him a nice edge. That way he could survive much worse.

Fredric veered off the highway and biked a half-mile along a quiet road to an office park. He sped through an intersection just as the light turned red and smiled. A last burst of freedom before joining the grind.

With the skyline of Munich visible in the distance, Fredric approached a building that resembled a random distribution center. It had no signs on the outside. Only a few windows dotted the façade of the building, and they were lined with bars. Nothing made the building notable enough to draw attention.

Fredric pedaled along the fence surrounding the perimeter of the building and its parking lot, which was filled with cars. The fence was the biggest giveaway that the building was somehow different from any others in this industrial complex. That, and all the cars. *If only more people biked to work like I do,* it occurred to him *there wouldn't be so many cars in the parking lot.*

Fredric biked up to the little guard station at the parking lot entrance and flashed his ID. The guard waved hello, and the guard rail lifted so he could wheel on through. He drove up to a nondescript door and unclipped his shoes from the bike. He carried the bike over one shoulder as he walked in, making loud clicks on the floor with the large cleats on the bottom of the cycling shoes. He looked askance at a discarded candy bar wrapper, a glaring omission in this spotless place.

He stared ahead to the clear plastic barrier. *I wish the plastic doors could just sense me coming and slide forward.* He walked halfway through a turnstile, setting off a blue light flashing on the clear plastic side walls. He took off his sunglasses and stared down into a black box with a clear plastic cover. He then scanned his ID badge over a reader. Quickly, the doors opened.

On the wall inside, the logo of an outstretched bird with the words *Bundesnachrichtendienst* circling it hung prominently on the wall. This phrase stood for the German intelligence agency BND.

He was heading to the building's gym to shower and change when he saw a man twenty years older, dressed in a turtleneck sweater and sports coat, stood stiffly waiting for him.

Walter Schneider barked tonelessly, "Come to my office as soon as you can. We are going to have a meeting there in twenty minutes." He regarded the bicycle with distaste. "By the way, you'll be flying out tonight, so you better stow that securely."

"Is this a formal meeting or just you and me?" Fredric asked.

Schneider did not answer the question. "Go," he coldly replied.

You'd get more love out of a stone, Fredric thought as he went downstairs to the gym to shower and get ready. He was a stocky six-footer with a square face, piercing blue eyes, and short black hair. He didn't take care of his body like he used to. He had built his well-developed chest and arm muscles, and equally thick thighs, in the German armed forces. But for the past few years he'd been hitting the bottle, leading to a faint beer belly.

Within twenty minutes, he was dressed in a pair of crisp blue jeans and a heavy black sweater. He went to his small office cubicle and tossed his gym bag under his desk. Unsleeping his computer to check for messages, he saw "Zhivago," a jazz tune by Kurt Rosenwinkel, still mounted on the screen.

As he entered the cramped office of his boss, he was the only one not carrying a pen or pencil. He didn't need one as his ability to recall details precisely was unrivaled by any one of the spies in the room. His boss was sitting at his conference table with two senior-level officials. Fredric pulled up a chair and sat down, directly facing his boss, looking for cues of what might be happening. *He looks uncomfortable,* Fredric thought.

"We have a new job for you, Fredric. Budapest. Tonight. And, it's exactly your type of assignment—one where you get complete freedom to carry out the mission without worrying about guidance on how to proceed from us."

Fredric ignored the sarcasm. "Oh, I get it. Send me off to Budapest in the dead of winter. This is a punitive assignment, because of that blown tip in Hamburg?" His soft, airy voice belied his intimidating presence.

Walter Schneider shook his head. "We really do need you for this assignment. You're good with numbers, with tech. We have a possible disaster on our hands, and I want you to find out what the hell is going on. Do you think you can manage that?"

Barbara Nahles, a special assistant to the agency director, spoke up. "Have you been paying attention to the civil disorder in Kenya?"

Fredric nodded, not sure what this was supposed to mean to him.

"What happened there poses a significant potential risk for Germany's economy. It looks like the problem started as a brazen attack in cyberspace. Only these weren't just hackers. Their well-organized attack quickly destabilized the government. Germany could be next. We need you to figure out who is responsible and why."

She shuffled through several file folders in front of her. "Here it is," she finally remarked. "Here is the report on the situation: 'After the cyber-attack, no one could access the funds on their accounts because their phones showed that the balance was zero. People could not pay for their groceries because merchants said that there was no money on their cellphone account. Even large corporations in Kenya were shocked to find that the balance in their domestic bank accounts was zero, where there would normally be millions in cash reserves."

She continued reading. "The International Monetary Fund (IMF) has offered to discuss options to aid the government to help keep its financial house together. The major cellphone company, which is owned by a large telecommunications giant in London, issued a statement: 'Everyone will be made whole soon. We will issue service credits and waive fees for everyone who was impacted. We are finding the source of the issues impacting our operations in Kenya and will resolve them soon. We will make everyone whole.'"

She chuckled and everyone laughed. That was obviously a load of PR nonsense.

Fredric asked, "Question one: who benefits from what is happening? And that leads me to question two, why Budapest should be my starting point."

Schneider took back the reins. "The signals intelligence group in Department 2 flagged some chatter coming from gamers in Budapest in the days leading up to the breakdown in Kenya.

It got on their radar screen because the phrases and words they were using triggered the algorithm we use. They were suggesting something big would happen. The chatter wasn't clear. Those same gamers then hijacked mainframes of telecommunications companies in Kenya and took them offline. The main guy they were watching said he was booking a flight to Berlin. Maybe Berlin was a code name. You know, it could be the proxy for the city that they were flying to. But we don't know for sure."

"Video gamers?" Fredric asked with raised eyebrows.

"Yes. Our unit that focuses on cyber-surveillance uses online games to identify bad guys. You know, virtual community-based games like World of Warcraft, EverQuest, or SecondLife. They are perfect covers for evil actors because everyone is already using an assumed identity. Not to mention that many gamers use person-to-person transfer services to transfer money fast."

"You mean, the deep web," Fredric said, referring to sites where criminals could buy and sell everything imaginable and pay for it anonymously. "The network of websites uses encryption and other techniques to allow users to surf with complete anonymity."

Heads were nodding.

"Are these suspicions collaborated with any other indications of a pending attack on our country? Our cyber defenses have to be better than some third world country like Kenya," Fredric remarked.

Nahles quickly jumped in. "Whoever did this was very sophisticated. They were accessing the internet in a way that our best technical spies have not been able to penetrate." Fredric did not know much about the complex world of encryption. He knew about old tricks like masking a real IP address by using a distorting proxy server. "Think of what they pulled off," she went on. "Thousands of accounts were drained of their funds, and we have no way of tracking where they all went to. But we are fairly confident that the host computer our team has been tracking is in Budapest, and the linguists are fairly certain that the person is of Eastern European origin, based on the instant messages sent among the people involved with the communications. We have no more specifics on who they are. No promising leads on addresses. No ideas on affiliations. No leads. We need you to work sources on the ground there. Our cyber-intelligence specialists tell me that what they can find and learn suddenly dried up. This could be the proverbial calm before the storm."

Fredric's eyes got wide. "Who will benefit from this? Then, let's determine who could pull off a heist of this magnitude. Forget for a moment what country they are in. What you are telling me suggests the people involved have sophisticated technical skills, so you aren't talking about simply a couple or small handful of people. What non-state actors could do something like this? They will leave a trail that leads right to them that they think no one will be able to find."

Schneider stirred uneasily in his seat. He was like a lot of old-timers Fredric knew: he had learned what he could about cyberspace, but technical know-how did not come naturally to him. His boss finally spoke. "We all have seen the headlines about the organizations that have had security breaches that resulted in people's most sensitive information being stolen. Health-care providers. Retailers. Banks. Investment companies. Utilities. Schools. Those behind these attacks often are found, but even on that level, sometimes they aren't . Or, they get indicted and live safely in countries that have no intention of extraditing their citizens to the West to stand trial. This is more than just a run of the mill breach or the petty industrial espionage case that the Americans are always blaming on Chinese military hackers. It is on the level of the military-grade internet attacks that damaged Iran's nuclear devices a few years ago. That's what makes it so urgent that we find who is responsible, because no one knows who might be next." Schneider added, unnecessarily, "Use your good judgment and do whatever you need to do. If you do anything stupid, you are on your own."

This briefing was not giving him a lot to go on. That was not entirely displeasing, since that meant he could make his own choices as he went along.

A secretary was already looking up flights from Munich to Budapest. As if on cue, she came in holding an iPad. "You are flying Tarom Airlines with a layover in Bucharest." Unspoken was the BND's desire to avoid any nonstop flights that might tip off anyone who wanted to figure out if a German agent had come to Budapest. "I will be right back with a printout of your flight itinerary."

The flight was scheduled to depart in three hours, so he got up and left the conference room to go back to his cubicle. He reached into a drawer and laid out his real German passport, a stack of four other passports held together with a rubber band, several hard-plastic components, a nail, some underwear, and a few pieces of paper. He opened another cabinet and retrieved a small box of clear hard plastic pieces that even most people in his profession could be forgiven for thinking looked like bullets. He put them in a faded green and black backpack that showed signs of wear on the sides. He added a few well-worn jeans and turtleneck sweaters.

He stopped by BND's finance office to pick up a wad of Hungarian forint, because he would use mainly cash once in Budapest. He also received several prepaid debit cards that he could use for his lodging and other needs.

He reported in to Schneider, and as he turned to walk out, his boss said, "Let me come with you. Even though we really don't have a clear lead, between me and you, this has the scale and sophistication of Srepska written all over it. Keep an open mind, but if you ever reach a dead end, look for a Srepska connection. And if you need help, the code word for this project is the series of phrases that involves a lock.

"That's going to be quite a mouthful," Fredric joked, even though he knew Schneider had no sense of humor whatsoever.

Fredric thought back to what he had heard secondhand in recent years about Srepska. To his own way of thinking, others within the German government, such as in law enforcement, were better suited to look into any hypothetical connection between Srepska and what happened in Kenya. He recalled a friend telling him how Americans were fascinated by organized crime families that operated sophisticated yet seemingly untouchable operations in major cities during the Prohibition era. He didn't know much else, but wondered how, as one man, he could be expected to make much progress with a well-developed and sophisticated crime ring. Why would he be assigned to work alone on such a herculean task?

Yet he knew the answer: *in case they need to throw me to the wolves.*

CHAPTER 3

THE NEXT MORNING, Fredric woke up to the alarm on his phone. It played a new song from Joachim Schoenecker, a guitarist he had recently discovered. The hotel room was chic modern, or at least a cheap version of it. He splashed cold water against his face, as he had done many times before to fight hangovers. He did his routine of jumping jacks, then waved his short hair back with water.

He took the elevator to the lobby, then headed to the dining area, where he saw mainly businesspeople eating breakfast. He scanned the many pillars in the breakfast area, each of which had a light on them. The lights were not needed because of the light blazing in from the large windows. White tablecloths barely covered the tables, yet were neatly hung in a decorative way.

He was at first surprised that the waiter guarding the buffet breakfast bar greeted him *good morning* in German, but he immediately switched to English to converse. That had happened before, waiters assuming he was German. He thought through his briefing as he ate. *If these people really pulled off that scam in Kenya*, he thought, *I surely am not the only person trying to find them.*

After breakfast, he walked along the Danube promenade, heading to the Hungarian Ministry of the Interior. A cold breeze from the river slapped his face, bringing the unpleasant smell of an urban waterway. In passing he studied the soaring arches of a Gothic church, then the Baroque grandeur of other buildings along the way. They housed many cafes and restaurants and boutiques selling designer clothes.

He finally ended up at a Rococo five-story building overlooking the river. He told the security guard, "I'm here to see Janos Nagy."

"Is he expecting you?"

"No, but if you ring him, you'll find that he will meet with me on short notice."

He produced a German passport that featured his picture but the name of Miles Duselmann. "Tell him that his old buddy Fritz is here to see him."

Janos Nagy was the Director-General of Hungary's TEK, responsible for Hungary's counter-terrorism efforts. He was working in his corner office on the top floor when his secretary's voice came over the intercom. When she told him what his guest's name was, he told her quickly, "Why yes, show him up."

Fredric soon sauntered into the office, holding his coat over one shoulder, dressed in the same casual black jeans and a sweater that he had worn the day before.

"Good to see you, Fritz," Nagy said, coming out from behind his desk. The large office was filled with Hungarian patriotic memorabilia: a large flag, pictures of troops from old wars, and a bust of a former Hungarian leader. Given the way the sun was reflecting off the stone, Fredric couldn't make out the name. The door was shut by the secretary who had guided Fredric into the office.

"It's been a long time. Twenty years goes by so fast. What are you doing these days?"

"I thought you knew me better than to have to ask that," Fredric said with a laugh. "Same thing. And here you have exited the business and started a new career. Well, maybe not a new career, since you are obviously using your old skills, but you have moved up the ladder."

Fredric looked at Nagy's watch and noticed it had dozens of diamonds, not to mention being encased in white gold. Life as a bureaucrat must be good, he thought. Back in the late 1990s, he and Nagy had teamed up in war-torn Chechnya. They met working on a mission to find radioactive cesium containers. Back then, they were NATO members trying to track down potential "dirty bomb" ingredients that were stolen during the chaos after the fall of the former Soviet Union. NATO suspected these containers had been shipped to Chechnya, to groups aligned with Islamic extremists.

"Naturally, of course," Nagy responded, warming to the times they'd shared together. "Remember, we were only supposed to do fact-finding, yet we caught that lead that brought us to where the stolen Radium-226 was being held for a buyer. Neither of us would have succeeded had we not worked together." The two shared a look, because they both knew what he really meant. Fredric had saved his life on the war-torn streets of Grozny. Nagy quickly corrected himself: "I wouldn't be here had you not taken out the sniper that day."

Fredric dismissed the old memory, not wanting to make too much of it. "So, do you really like this job? I can't imagine a more tedious existence than having to wake up every morning and go to the same office every day, go home, and know that tomorrow will be exactly like today."

"I see you haven't lost the ability to speak your mind, Fredric," Nagy replied dryly.

Nagy whirled around in his chair to his office refrigerator and retrieved a bottle of American bourbon. He poured it into two small glasses on top of the refrigerator and set them on the conference table. Fredric pulled out a chair as Nagy motioned to him and remarked, "Have a seat."

The two men drank to old times, then to future times.

"That's good stuff," Fredric said as he read the label: Hudson

Baby Bourbon. The deceptively plain bottle alone told him it was well outside his price range.

"Fredric, are you still living in that industrial area in Munich— remind me of the name?"

"Obergiesing. Yes, it's still my base, but living there may be too strong of a word."

"Is your father still alive? I recall you and he were close, right?"

"Actually, no, I haven't spoken to him much since he divorced my mom. If you remember, he worked in a steel mill in Munich before he went to work as a miner in Austria. He married a woman half his age when I was only four. I haven't seen him in a long, long time. I do know he is alive, just because I'm a snoop."

"Sorry, Fredric, I remembered that wrong," Nagy said. "I thought it was your dad who got you into this line of work, but..."

"That was my stepdad, Lothair." His mother had married the man a day after his thirteenth birthday. Unlike his father, he had visited them last Christmas, celebrating in the home they had owned since they got married. Lothair was too strict and bossy for a stepfather, but Fredric had to admit that he never would have entered the military if not for Lothair.

He soon steered the talk to his present business. "Tell me, what groups have the ability to pull off a well-coordinated cyber-attack? I'm not talking about a company. I mean an entire nation, like Kenya. Do you have a database of cyber criminals I could look at?" Fredric asked.

Nagy furrowed his brow and replied, "All the Western govern-ments think Eastern Europe is the hotbed of hackers, but this is not necessarily true here in Hungary. If you can be more specific about what you are trying to find out and why, I might be able to help you."

Fredric was wary of open-ended requests. "Okay, I under-stand," he said, watching Nagy closely. "The name I was given was Srepska. What do you know about them?"

Nagy abruptly set down the liquor glass with a thump. He stiffened visibly in his chair. He had been so talkative before, but now he clammed up completely. Fredric could tell that he had struck a nerve, and that made him perplexed. Nagy used to be all about bringing culprits to justice.

The look on his face changed to one of fear. Fredric had to wonder what he was going up against if a powerful figure in law enforcement in Hungary became afraid when this group was mentioned.

"You are a friend and I owe you a tremendous debt. My life, for that matter. But I really cannot help you with respect to Srepska or this Kenya matter," he said breathlessly. "You can expect no help from me whatsoever."

Fredric was eyeing him curiously. Maybe life behind a desk had eroded his friend's former courage. "That's fine, I understand. I will work some other leads," he calmly replied.

Nagy continued. "You really should not pursue this lead. If they discover you are on their trail, they will have no compunction about killing you. I mean it. There isn't anything I can do to protect you."

Fredric was trying to puzzle out what this all meant. Did Srepska contain former or even active members of the Hungarian intelligence agency? Was that why Nagy was covering up for them? Thoughts of betrayal crossed his mind as he saw the pained look on Nagy's face. From now on he would have to watch his back with Nagy too.

"Let me get this straight. You don't know anything about Srepska, you don't know who they are, or you don't want to help me?"

"Fredric, my friend, if I could help you, I would. But I am not at liberty to discuss it further. You really need to leave this office now."

"You know me. I don't run that easily," Fredric said, showing a confident smile. He calmly lifted his coat off his chair. "I understand that you cannot or will not help me, but it was still good to see you, old friend."

Fredric shook hands with Nagy and walked out of his office. Yet he had no intention of leaving. Instead he sat down in a chair in the outer office and proceeded to open his backpack. Feeling the secretary's eyes on him, he made a show of pulling out his phone and checking it for texts. He was merely buying time. He leaned forward slightly, until he could see Nagy's form through the doorway.

As he had expected, he saw Nagy standing up, talking on the phone with a furrowed brow and waving his arm.

I wish I could hear, Fredric thought. *Should I go in and pretend I left something?*

He made a show of patting his coat, then checking the pockets. He shrugged helplessly to the secretary. "I forget things all the time. My wife says that if my head wasn't attached to my neck, I'd walk around like a chicken."

When she smiled benevolently, he headed back into the office. Of course, there was no wife. He loathed the very notion of it.

Fredric strode in confidently. "Excuse me, did I leave my scarf here?" he asked while glancing up at Nagy.

Nagy instantly clicked off the phone and set it down. *He looks shocked to see me. He looks nervous. That's not like him.*

"My scarf, did you see it?" he asked.

Nagy finally found his voice. "Not here, my friend. You probably left it at the guard's desk when you first came. Check with them."

Fredric politely thanked him before walking out.

So, who was Nagy calling? Why did he look like he was in a panic? Fredric didn't know the answers yet, but he had nailed down one point. He was in the right place.

CHAPTER 4

FREDRIC HEADED BACK to his hotel. He pored over in his mind every moment of his visit with Nagy, particularly Nagy's uncharacteristic nervousness and newfound costly tastes. Even the head of the anti-terrorism outfit couldn't be making much of a salary.

He spotted an internet café in the subterranean floor of a building as he was walking. Going down a few stairs, he plopped down money for time on a computer and a coffee. "Can I plug my flash drive into your computer so I can use Tor?" he asked louder than his normal conversational voice. The Tor browser ensured that no one could trace back to the computer he was using.

"Of course," came the reply from an annoyed clerk who was more interested in scrolling through Facebook on her smartphone. Fredric, aware of everything around him at all times, also noticed the two younger men standing nearby behind the counter, their heads buried in their phones. The mention of "Tor" didn't seem to affect them.

He ran searches on the deep web, using Tor. He was frustrated at the slow speed of the browser. He eventually accessed a site where he used the screen name *Furtim* to post an advertisement that only others using this browser could find. He quickly skimmed ads to see the current selling price for stolen credit card numbers in the area. He then posted a message on a forum advertising the availability of stolen magnetic tape storage devices, containing backups of account information for customers of H&K Bank. He wrote that they were available for sale to the highest bidder willing to make the trade in Budapest.

He searched other sites as well where stolen financial records were available, or experts were selling their technological services to break the law for the right fee. He wasn't trying to gather useful intelligence. He just hoped that others in the café would see him browse sites commonly used to traffic in illegal goods.

After half an hour, he asked the young man at the front desk, "Do you know who might be hiring a guy who is proficient at computer networks and getting his clients' job done? I am new in town and looking for a job." He smiled, portraying what he said next. "It's time for me to stop trafficking in stolen credit cards. Do you have any leads?"

"Not here," came the reply from an indifferent voice.

He then asked for a suggestion of a good bar to go to that evening…one the locals would go to. His intent was not so much to drink, as it was to listen and chat up others. Sticking his hand in the lion's den was the only way he was going to stir up results.

He repeated this routine at two other cafes, planning to return to each. All the while he checked his email for anyone offering to purchase the goods he had for sale. At each cafe, he scanned who was using the computers, keeping them in mind for his return visits. It was a long shot, but others might be using an anonymous café for the same reason he was.

He grabbed a gyro and soda and headed back to his hotel. Once upstairs in his room, he opened his backpack and pulled out several hard-plastic components. He put them on the table. Aligning them carefully, he snapped the components together. He soon had a small firearm that easily fit within his hand. He loaded into it several plastic bullets. He would have to buy other firepower if he developed any leads, but this would serve his immediate purposes.

He then opened his computer to research the British cellphone company whose network had crashed. He began typing out a list of all the functions that the cellphone company would need to operate, and the names of the businesses they worked with that he could find out through online searches, such as power companies, information technology consultants, external auditors, lenders, and computer hardware suppliers.

Ninety minutes later, he heard a small thump outside his door. He quickly reached to his ankle and pulled out his small plastic handgun. He slipped off his chair and took cover next to the bed. He waited several seconds, until he was convinced that no one was trying to open the door. He then got up and slowly headed over.

He found a large envelope lying in the hallway outside. *I don't see any wires. Good, it's going to be a clue for me to work with and not a bomb.* He picked up the envelope and quickly retreated, closing the door again. He examined the package before opening it, feeling for any wires or the like that would set off a bomb upon opening it. All he felt was flatness. Opening it up, he found it contained a single piece of paper on which an address was handwritten: 36 Kiraly Street.

Fredric sat back in his chair. He knew Nagy from their time working on joint undercover assignments. The two had shared a studio apartment and gotten to know each other quite well. The note wasn't in his handwriting, and it was unlikely that he would have come to the hotel to deliver the note himself because he might be recognized. Still, this looked like his handiwork. He was relieved that his old friend hadn't gone over completely to the dark side.

He placed a call to the German embassy in Budapest and soon was speaking with the lead resident BND intelligence operative. "A friend has supplied a key," Fredric said.

There was a long pause. "When should we expect delivery?" came the reply.

Fredric said, "Let me get back to you on that. In the meantime, I could really use a locksmith."

Fredric used his phone to map the address Nagy had supplied. Wanting the exercise, Fredric walked the two miles to the location. Along the way, the bass line from "Vulcan Princess" hummed in his head. As a teen, Fredric played the drums, much to the displeasure of his migraine-prone mother and her delicate, classically trained eardrums. Though she worked as a seamstress, she was a talented musician who once dreamed of becoming a concert pianist. After she insisted that he quit the drums, he transferred his passion to bass guitar. He grew to love jazz, and for a few years Eberhard Weber was his idol. He still kept up, checking out club schedules. If he stuck around long enough, he could check out the scene in Budapest.

He soon arrived at a large white one-story A-frame house with closed brown blinds. He glanced up at the copper roof, turned green from atmospheric conditions. He glanced down at the narrow windows for the basement. A fence ran around the perimeter, with overgrown trees and other shrubbery that made it difficult to see the house. A quick scan of the patio showed no chairs or toys or other signs that would mark a Hungarian family. It looked like a rental property that was badly managed. A place the neighbors shunned. In other words, a good place for an illegal operation.

He took out his phone and called back the BND operative at the embassy. "I am suddenly having a bad ringing in my ears. I think I may be sick. Where is the nearest clinic to the tea house at Kazinczy and Dob streets?" Fredric asked as he thought back to a small yet busy café he had passed by earlier.

"I need to find a map and get back to you," his contact said.

Satisfied that he had called for reinforcements, Fredric went to a local market and purchased a bag of pretzels. He munched on them as he took another stroll around the neighborhood. No one was out in the streets, other than a couple stray dogs that crossed his path along the way. He headed back and lingered a block away from the tea house, watching the passersby.

A half hour later, he observed a skinny man who looked barely twenty-one, holding a map with a headset. He immediately recognized from the prearranged clues that the man was his contact. Yet he had to wonder if this operative had enough experience to be helpful. *Maybe only teenagers know tech in this country.*

He walked up to the young man, who was fumbling with his map, and used the day's catch phrase: "Where can you find a good tailor?"

The young man responded, "Go south two blocks, then east."

Fredrick nodded, and they casually walked away from the café. "I am Istvan," the man said. "What do you need?"

"I have a lead on a house a few blocks from here that I want to investigate. I want to know who lives in it, how long they have lived there, what they do for a living, and who they are talking to. I want to know what is going on in there now."

"No problem," Istvan replied in English that had a noticeable Hungarian accent. "I have all the supplies I need in my car. It is a perfect time now that it is getting dusk. That will give me the cover I need."

Istvan and Fredric silently walked to his car, several blocks away. The four-door light yellow Skoda Favorit looked at least fifteen years old. He approached and unlocked the driver's side door. He got in and reached over and unlocked the passenger's door for Fredric. The first thing that Fredric saw was all the snack food wrappers and soda bottles strewn throughout the car, along with a backseat full of what looked to be random junk such as books, flower containers, and plastic bags. *Is this part of the disguise or is the kid a total slob?*

"Okay, tell me again what we need to do," Istvan asked.

"The house I need to monitor is 36 Kiraly Street. And you can call me Fritz."

"Okay, let's drive by it and check it out," Istvan said as he started the car.

"How long have you been doing this?" Fredric asked casually, like he was just making conversation.

"I have been working in IT since before I started secondary school," he said. "I graduated and began working for a friend of my dad's who had a security business. He has a military background and a really good reputation, so the BND became interested in me."

Fredric guessed that he probably was working with someone technically qualified. Whether Istvan had the guts to do what Fredric wanted was still an open question.

"It's the house on the right," Fredric announced, looking straight ahead as they passed by the house.

"Okay, the telephone junction box is right there at the end of the block," Istvan said. "What do the Americans say? Easy-peasy. Let's park around the corner."

Easy-peasy, Fredric grumbled to himself. *Where do they get these people?*

They got out and Istvan opened the trunk. "Here, put on this vest so you look like an employee of Magyar Telekom. That's the big phone company here," he said as he handed Fredric a vest with a pink T. Istvan grabbed a small backpack and they headed for the junction box.

Istvan took a tool out of his backpack and used it to loosen a bolt on the front of the box. He then lifted off the cover, revealing a bundle of wires inside, dozens of wires, some red and green, others yellow and black. He ran his fingers along the cable coming into the junction box from below. He followed the wires to where they were plugged into a panel. He looked carefully at the circuit board that the wires were plugged into. He found one that had the number 36 written next to the wire port. He removed the insulation and reached into his backpack to grab a small black device.

He then affixed to it the wire. With some black electrical tape, he wrapped the small device tightly to the phone wire.

Meanwhile, Fredric was furtively looking around for anyone who might be paying attention to them. A car drove by, but the driver didn't look their way. Why would anyone look at telephone repairmen?

Then Istvan took out of his backpack a thick box with an accompanying antenna, about the size of a book. He lifted the bundle of wires and jammed the device into the phone box. He then put the cover back on. "Let's go," he told Fredric.

As they walked back to the car, Fredric's feeling about the operation was looking up. The kid seemed to be a real pro. Fredric started to feel that pleasant burr in his chest when the game was afoot.

"You have heard of Stingrays, right?" Istvan said, and Fredric nodded. "The one I used was the brand-new cousin, much smaller than the one the police use, yet it can capture all cellphone traffic in its range even better than the bigger ones. It's an absolute beauty. It can break the phone's encryption so we can read any text messages being sent or received on the phone. We just need to be within about a two-mile radius of it to monitor what it finds."

Fredric was cautiously optimistic. He was aware that the cutting-edge gadget tricked cellphones into thinking it was a cellphone tower. That would allow them to monitor the cellphone conversations and plot on a map where the phones were being used.

After a short pause, Istvan said, "And remember that smaller two-inch black box that I plugged into one of the open phone jacks? Well, that little gizmo will transfer all the information we intercept to my cellphone." He glanced over with a wry smile. "It would be scary if the police had the same technology we do."

"All right. Well, let's open it up and see what we get."

CHAPTER 5

THEY WEREN'T GOING to stay in the car, where they'd be sitting ducks if anyone inside the house realized their communications were being intercepted. "We should go somewhere we can work without others watching or hearing us," Istvan said. "And, ideally a place with electricity because this will probably take a while."

"How about we work in my hotel room?" Fredric said. "I don't mind listening around the clock to what's going on in the house. If you can get me set up, we can take shifts."

"Sounds like a plan," Istvan said, and added nonchalantly, "As long as I can use the room service."

"It's a deal. We'll bill the government. After all, they would want to feed a growing young boy."

As they were driving, both removed their phone company vests. Fredric followed Istvan's lead of stashing it below his seat. Soon, Istvan pulled over and they parked. As they walked back to Fredric's hotel, the sun was getting low in the sky. He was eager to discover what sort of chatter they'd turn up.

Fredric pushed aside the glass panel of the revolving front door. "Let's go up and get to work."

Istvan followed Fredric's lead, walking authoritatively to the elevator. They went up to the fifth floor and headed down the hallway. "This is my room," Fredric pointed.

Immediately upon entering his room, Fredric froze. The double beds were turned sideways, and the drawers of the cabinets had been pulled out. Two of the sofa's cushions were lying haphazardly on the floor and one was on top of the bed. A single unfired bullet taped to the television caught his eye.

Someone wanted to scare him away—someone, he thought, contacted by the Hungarian TEK.

Fredric pulled out his gun, though it looked like whoever did this was long gone. Istvan had a frozen look on his face, trying to conceal his fright.

Fredric searched his clothes and other personal items that he had taken out of his backpack when he got to the room and realized that none of them gave any clue of what he was up to. Luckily, he had his tablet computer in his backpack.

"Let's go," he announced to Istvan. As they walked down the hall, he said, "They know I am here. I don't want anything to happen to you. After I leave, I want you to leave, but take a different exit. They are after me, not you, but you still need to watch your back. Let's reconvene in two hours near where you parked your car. If either of us even thinks we are being followed, then we will try to meet up tomorrow instead. Where could we meet where we could blend in with a lot of people?"

Istvan replied in a nervous, shaky voice, "Let's meet at seven at the Great Market Hall. It will be easy for you to find, and lots of people will be there for supper. There is a stairwell that leads from the main floor to the top floor. We can meet at the stairwell in the center of the Market on the first floor."

"Deal. Stay safe. I will go out the front door. You should try to leave through the back door, or else linger in the stairwell and then leave a few minutes later."

Fredric then took the elevator to the first floor.

"Change in plans," he told the receptionist downstairs. "I have to head out of town unexpectedly," he said at the top of his conversational voice as the front desk attendant looked unamused. "I am checking out. By the way, you need to do a better job of security because someone broke into my room. They trashed the place. And I hope you won't be charging me for my stay here, given what happened. I better not see a charge on my credit card."

The concierge looked shocked. "Are you serious? Let me call security," she said as she reached for her phone. He noticed her hand was shaking.

"No, I have had it." He tossed his key on the counter and turned around to leave. "Your management is going to be hearing about this from me. No business traveler should have to put up with this outrage."

As he stepped out on the sidewalk, a grin appeared on his face. Those poor morons at the front desk. But then he heard the door of a car gently close behind him. Turning slightly, he noticed a young man emerge from a parked car that he had just passed. He looked lot like Istvan except he was shorter. He was wearing a black stocking cap and a black jacket.

Fredric kept walking. *There would be nothing more embarrassing than being shot in the back, and I am not going to let that happen.* He looked back out of the corner of his eye and saw that the man was still behind him.

Fredric walked to a square fronting the Hungarian parliament building and thought of entering, until he saw a long line at the ticket office. As he cast about for another ruse, his eyes stopped on a big stone obelisk with a five-pointed star on top. It looked out of place surrounded by grand old buildings. Several groups of tourists were scattered around the monument as a guide was explaining the meaning of the monument in English. "It is a memorial to the Soviet Army troops who occupied our city during the latter part of World War II. Many older people don't care for this monument because it reminds them of the Soviet occupation."

A few moments later, he saw a smiling vaguely familiar face

in bronze. It was Ronald Reagan, who he remembered as a former American president. He walked down the pedestrian walkway running parallel to the Danube River. Everything, from the recently refurbished pavement to the cash machine built into a medieval city wall, was shiny and new. He noticed how fancy the storefronts looked, yet the buildings housing them looked ancient.

Fredric turned left, and he immediately saw the Basilica of St. Stephen. He went up its steps and pretended to enjoy the view of the city while noticing that the person following him was lingering below. The man in the black cap was fumbling with his shoe, trying not to look suspicious. Yet Fredric knew that he was the stranger's target. He also knew the man wanted him alive. That meant he had to bring him in, and Fredric had no intention of letting that happen.

As Fredric continued walking, he glanced behind him and saw the same man a block back. He started walking down random streets, and sure enough, the tail followed faithfully along. Once he saw that the man talking on a cellphone, nodding his head as though taking orders, Fredric immediately headed toward the central train terminal, Keleti.

He walked halfway around the nineteenth-century station, staring at the four six-foot tall statues parallel to a large semicircle. It was so much larger than the terminal in Berlin. He climbed the steps toward the main entrance and pushed his shoulder hard against the heavy glass door. He felt as if he were entering a cathedral. The space in front of him echoed with sound, not just from speakers but from trains. Large pillars and wall paintings gave the impression of a vast chamber where aristocrats held their balls.

He glanced at the board and ran through the list of trains going to various local towns, most of which he had never heard of. Fredric waited in line before the ticket booths. Like the building itself, the ticket office featured highly decorated, elaborately designed wooden counters freshly painted with a shiny coat of lacquer.

When it came his turn at the window, he asked what time the next train was running to Zagreb, Croatia. He thanked the clerk and left, never having any intention of going there. He was simply buying time to identify who else might be following him and craft an exit plan. He went back outside.

The person following him was nowhere to be seen, but that didn't mean anything. By this time, a second tail might be watching him. He began walking. He unzipped his backpack, took out a latex glove and slipped it on his right hand. He reached in his backpack again and emerged with a large mitten for his left hand. Now his special surprise was all set.

After walking for another ten minutes, the man reappeared. And now not one but three people, keeping a safe distance, followed him through every turn. The merry chase was on.

He reached a large traffic circle with a tall columned monument in the center. Statues of famous military leaders wearing swords stood between columns. He idly wondered how useless he would be in his work if all he had at his disposal was a sword. He entered a park, and after a short journey through the trees, he saw yet another strange building with a combination of styles. Every tower had a different shape. Around this strange castle was a pond, and a giant gothic arch with spiked bars could be lowered to bar unwanted visitors. A nearby sculpture attracted his attention, one with a monk with the hood over his face.

He kept walking. Now only two men were behind him. He wondered what happened to the first man. Maybe he had veered off in another direction.

He left the buildings behind until he reached a remote, wild section, filled with trees and ravines that made it difficult to see. He scanned the horizon and saw no one else besides the two people he knew who were following him. This looked like a good spot to confront them.

He found a stone archway that presented a suitable hiding spot. He slipped in behind the mortared stones, slightly damp and lightly covered with an odd yellowed mildew, like tree droppings. He had to be prepared to overpower them and ask questions. His blood was pumping as he lay in wait. He felt ready for these two goons. If they were part of Srepska, maybe they were techies assigned to a thug's job. They were no match for him, at any rate.

As they approached the archway, he noticed that the guy on the left was wearing a red jacket and beige slacks and had a full black beard. The clean-shaven, bigger guy on the right wore a black jacket and blue jeans and had short cropped hair. With that menacing look on his face, he didn't look like he spent too much time in front of a computer screen.

"Can I help you?" Fredric said loudly, stepping out when they were still a safe distance away, far enough that they couldn't tackle him.

"What are you doing here?" the shorter man said, clearly startled.

"You are going to regret poking around in our lovely city," the taller one said as he took out a metal pipe. "We know why you are here, and that's bad news for you."

Fredric assessed the two-foot pipe. A typical weapon for a street punk. As the shorter one reached behind his back toward his waist, Fredric's attention jumped away from the guy swinging the pipe. He knew everything was going down fast if a gun appeared. In the back of his mind he was still worried about being caught by surprise by the third man. Where had he gone?

The man pulled up something from his beltline behind his back and swung his arm around. Fredric's left hand then reached to the right and quickly took off the large oversize mitten. Revealed in his hand was a Walther P4, equipped with a menacing-looking silencer. This far out in the park, it would suppress the noise of the gun being fired enough.

Sure enough, the other man now had a gun in his hand.

"Put your gun down," the man with the pipe said as he raised his arm and began getting closer and closer.

"Why's that, Frankenstein?" Fredric said to buy time. "Are large people in your country afraid of guns?

He noticed the shorter man clicking off the safety of his gun. He read the faces on both of them—stone-cold. They must have orders, if all else failed, to kill him.

With a ruthless twist of his lips, he turned the Walther gun on the larger of the two. Almost in one motion he fired a double tap to his chest. In the next split second, he aimed at the other man, who had jerked back, stunned as his friend toppled clumsily to the ground.

Raising his revolver to shoulder height, Fredric still was hoping to get information out of the second one. He barked, "Let's talk."

But he could tell from the man's recovery he was shocked. Fredric answered with a single shot. The man's forehead suddenly blossomed with a third, red eye, slightly canted to the right. The man stood upright for several seconds, not aware that the back of his head had been blown off, then lost his footing and collapsed.

"You idiots," Fredric said in an agitated tone toward the fallen bodies. They were worth more to him alive than dead. "The Hussar warrior act doesn't work out so well sometimes, does it?"

He scanned the park again, worried that someone had seen what had just happened. No one was around. He had to flee the scene before anyone showed up. First, though, he quickly checked the pockets of the men he shot. He grabbed the IDs in their wallets and a business-card sized piece of paper. It appeared to be a list of numbers and possibly even passwords. He took several hundred forints, just to make it look like a robbery, along with a small walkie-talkie from each man's pocket. More valuable were their smartphones.

While crouching, he kept looking around the park. Despite the silencer, the muffled shots could have still drawn someone's attention. His collection duties completed, he rapidly walked away. As he neared the pond he had passed before, he slowed to his gait to that of a businessman hurrying back from lunch.

He waited until he left the park and traveled several blocks among the apartment buildings until he flipped open the phone of the man he first saw following him. He went to the call history section. He dialed the last number. A male voice answered with, "Is it done?" in Hungarian.

"Yes, they are, thanks for asking," Fredric replied in English, adding a British flair just to anger whoever it was. Any conflict he felt about shooting the two in cold blood slipped away. They really had been assigned to kill him.

He then quickly removed the batteries and SIM cards from the phones so they couldn't be tracked. He would pass them along to the BND so the data could be extracted.

At the next street corner, he tossed his plastic glove in a public trash can. He hesitated a moment with the mitten. The odd macabre touch it had added pleased him, and he didn't want to lose it. But then, sighing, he flung it in too. It wasn't hard to buy a mitten.

CHAPTER 6

"WHAT'S WRONG, KID?" the fit white-haired man shouted as two men sat across from him around a large wooden table. Liszt's *Piano Sonata in B minor* drowned out the hum of the racks of servers operating in the next room. Off in the corner was an empty black table on which sat a laptop, two computer screens, and several bottles of Soproni. Next to them were several circuit boards linked together with a USB cable. A steady breeze came through from the fans in the next room.

"Zoltan, something went horribly wrong," Mihaly said. His legs were visibly shaking and his voice cracked.

"What did you mess up now?" Zoltan said dismissively.

Mihaly sheepishly explained what happened in the park.

Suddenly there was silence. Istvan's face turned red. "How much do I have to pay to make sure this type of thing doesn't happen," Zoltan muttered.

"These were my friends. You are blaming me for them dying?"

"I couldn't care less about them. The biggest threat to our plans is that he is on the loose and you don't seem to be able to stop him."

Mihaly took a deep breath as he looked down at his heavily tattooed arms. He studied his latest tattoo, which to others looked to simply be Asian characters but to him was meant to bring him good luck—or at least his friend told him.

"I told you before, we are getting out of our league. Kenya drew unwanted attention."

Zoltan snapped, "You say that every time I try to push you in a new direction. And what happens each time?"

"But the guys I have worked with side by side for years are dead. It could have been me. We are dealing with some very sophisticated killer."

"Screw him," Zoltan scoffed. "Look how much money I've made you. You would be living out of your car if not for me. You want all that to be over?"

Angered, Zoltan rose from his chair. He picked up a coaster and hurled it on the floor in the direction of the doorway to the servers. Mihaly was jolted as the ceramic pieces scattered in all directions. Zoltan launched forward and grappled Mihaly by the neck and began shaking him. "This unknown operative and his friends could be about to walk through the door as we speak. Screw who's dead. Go find who did it and stop him. You know what will happen if you aren't successful," Zoltan said as Mihaly jerked back and forth.

"Go. You all have your work cut out for you," Zoltan said while waving his arm in the direction of several people in the room. Three men put on their leather jackets as they followed Mihaly out of the room.

Several minutes later, Zoltan heard the door in the adjoining room slam shut and the deadbolts slid across to secure it.

"Move faster with our plans," he shouted.

Despite the show of bravado he put up, he was worried. Someone who could kill two of his men, when it was two against one, smelled like a professional. From the description he'd received, this Fredric seemed to be German. Zoltan was not surprised. The chaos Srepska had caused in Africa was no secret. He had to keep moving swiftly to stay ahead of the packs of spies trying to find him.

Ahead of them was the big prize: The United States of America. That heist would dwarf the haul from Kenya.

"Bence!" he called, and a few moments later a skinny nerd with long shocks of black hair appeared. "Start shutting down the American ATMs now. We have to push forward before the vultures can swoop down on us."

CHAPTER 7

FREDRIC HAD WALKED for over an hour, staying clear of his hotel for the time being. Walking was a poor substitute for biking, but he liked the calming influence that aerobic exercise had on his heart. He found a delightful café, Peace in the Valley, that served some of the best red fish soup he had ever tasted. After his sojourn, he passed a small corner shop that had an air conditioner above the door and a display window filled with sweaters, hats, and shirts. He couldn't read Hungarian, but the word "Second" in the shop's name was painted on the display window. It looked like an upscale second-hand store. He walked in and noticed several pictures of men wearing casual clothes in the window. He scanned the small shop and realized he was the only customer.

An older female clerk quickly offered to help him. "*Segíthetek?*"

"I need a new casual outfit for my evenings in Budapest while I'm on my business trip. The airline lost my bag and I need some clothes for tonight while they find it. What would you suggest?"

He hated clothes shopping. He also hated asking for help, but knew he had to blend in with the locals. No more looking like a German.

She enthusiastically led him to a black and gray casual button-down shirt that felt thick and warm. She grabbed a black sweater and business-casual pants. The lady spoke little English and no German, so they communicated by pointing or trying to say phrases in broken English. After ten minutes, he returned to the sidewalk carrying a paper shopping bag with his old clothes folded inside.

He took a few right turns at each new corner, just to be sure that no one was following him. He still was wondering what happened to the third person. Was he just a spotter for the other two men?

He darted into an alleyway where no one was around. He crouched down in a doorway off the alleyway and zipped open his backpack. He pulled out a wig, and suddenly he sprouted a full head of black hair. He put on a pair of tinted glasses, as well as a small piece of skin-covered latex over his nose that resulted in a more squashed face. With his local clothing, he'd fool most observers.

He then found another hotel. The lobby was marked by garish lavender stripes that accented every horizontal surface. The female concierge had a uniform to match the décor. "I need a room for seven nights. What is the best rate that you can offer me?"

He checked in under a passport from the Netherlands with his picture, showing that his name was Dieter Kneoeff. "I like the pocket," he remarked, pointing at her blouse. "That color looks good on you."

She returned a smirk that showed him just how much she loved looking like the upholstery.

He walked up to his room on the second floor. Exhausted, he flopped down on the bed and promptly fell asleep. With his totally random choice of a hotel, he had no worries about being disturbed.

The next morning, he scanned the local news blogs and head-lines for any mention of what had happened in the park. Since nothing had been reported, he guessed that Srepska had cleaned up after him. They probably didn't want the police investigating the thugs' identities.

By now, he figured, he should be able to discover the fruits of his labors at the supposed Srepska location. Checking his phone, he confirmed where the Great Market Hall was. By design, yesterday's wanderings had ended up a few blocks away, and he soon entered the large brick building. He glanced around and saw dozens of small independent stores, set against the background of the several-story-tall black steel framed windows capped by a tall, angled roof. To prevent being trapped, he located the nearest exits, not an easy feat given the labyrinth of vendors. In addition to the door he came in, he saw an escalator but passed on finding where it would lead until he more fully surveyed the floor.

He soon spotted a stairway, and he breathed a sigh of relief as he saw Istvan standing there. He walked closer. *Does he really not see me?* Fredric wondered. Finally, their eyes met. Fredric made a movement with his chin as if to say *follow me*. He casually walked down the length of the historic market, continually scanning for anything amiss.

"Did you make sure you weren't followed coming here?" Fredric asked Istvan quietly as the two met. They blended in the throngs of people milling around at the shops, each having a specialty, whether it be meats, produce, or candies. Pleasingly, it resembled the bustle of Munich's outdoor farmers market.

"That was a real shocker back at the hotel, but I did exactly what you told me and no one seemed to notice that I existed. I kept checking and no one followed me yesterday, and nothing seemed weird today. That must have been tight for you. I was worried you weren't going to make it out of the hotel."

Fredric thought, if only his young accomplice knew what happened in the park after they parted ways.

"Let's pick up where we left off. I have a new hotel I am working out of." He took out his cellphone and scrolled to a page he had already preset. "This is the hotel," Fredric pointed. "Wait five minutes and go to Room 212 there."

Fredric walked back to the hotel. *What a nicely done planter,* he thought as he eyed in passing a four-foot wooden box with a lavender piano painted on the side.

Within five minutes, Fredric heard a knock.

Istvan walked in and from his backpack extracted his MacBook Air. He put ear buds in his ears and connected them to the laptop. Showing Fredric, he opened the Pen-Link and Lincoln software programs. After he connected a cord between his cellphone and the laptop, he clasped his hands and held them to his face. Fredric found he was tense, which made sense, since he had been waiting since the day before to discover if they'd hit the jackpot.

Then the young man pumped his fists in the air. "It was a success! I was able to connect to the device that we installed to monitor cellphone connections."

"The cellphones in the house?" Fredric asked.

"No, we still need to figure out what cellphones are associated with the house. There are a lot of cellphones connecting to our device."

Fredric gave a silent groan. "So how are you going to do it, then?"

"Well, I have a device that will listen for certain common financial terms. That should narrow down the search parameters."

That seemed workable. Fredric could record everything Istvan was collecting and get help to analyze it later.

Reaching into his bag, Istvan put an adapter on the audio outlet and plugged in another set of earbuds. "Here you can listen too," he motioned to Fredric while handing him the set.

They both listened in on the phone conversation for one line of calls. The communications were garbled.

"This line is encrypted," Fredric said.

The young man used the cursor on his computer to open a new program. "This one will try to break the encryption. It isn't easy and I don't usually have much success with it, but it is our only hope."

Fredric doubted that a preset program could break the code as it was running, but the very fact that the line was encrypted told him something. This phone was being used by someone who had something to hide.

"Can you record all of the communications that are on this encrypted cellphone line?" Fredric asked. He was convinced this was likely the one he needed to be tracking.

"Sure thing. Be patient, I have one more cool trick up my sleeve." Istvan switched to another program. "We are going to monitor the landline communications to and from the house." Just then a pop-up box appeared on the computer. "This means there is a phone call in process."

"It was an outgoing call to a number in London." Fredric jotted the number that appeared on the computer down on his notepad.

A man with a British accent answered. "We are ready for you to make the investment purchases," the second voice said.

"What did the boss finally decide on?" the British voice said.

"In the morning, make a two-million-dollar investment in the U.S. Dollar Bear Plus exchange traded fund on the Canadian stock exchange. And put another two million in the S&P 500 Bear 2X or any Financial Services Bear Fund. Then put four million in gold and silver. Lastly, buy three million worth of Chinese yuan. Fund these purchases with the cash balance in the account. And double-check to confirm that, as we discussed, none of our other investments have assets in the United States other than what we need for our current work there."

The call ended, and Fredric looked at Istvan. Fredric was thinking that the people he was listening to must have deep pockets and what was coming down the pike. "That's some pretty serious cash they're throwing around," Istvan echoed.

Fredric realized there was also internet traffic going over the phone line using DSL. "Do we have the software to view it?"

"No," Istvan sheepishly replied.

"Well then, make sure you are recording it so I can have someone analyze it." The technicians back in his agency had so many more sophisticated tools and advanced training on how to use them. "And start uploading some of these files so we can get them to start working."

Removing his headphones, Fredric ordered Hungarian veal stew and a salami platter via room service. Istvan had a burger. As they ate quietly, Fredric watched the computer program trying to break the encryption. He could only hope that the program would pop up and alert him to another landline call being made. He also had some options to view the DSL traffic.

"There are a lot of bytes of data being transferred here. I bet you someone is using the DSL line to conduct video chats," Istvan pointed out.

As they waited for more communications to erupt, Fredric found himself thinking about what had happened the day before. How did whoever hit his room know he was there? In hindsight, he was sure the visit to Nagy had been the trigger. Could Nagy's office have been under surveillance by someone who Nagy was fearful of offending yet powerless to stop? If this were the case, Nagy knew he was being watched. Perhaps he was responsible for the note, and the trip to install the device had saved his life because he was away from the hotel when these people had come looking for him. Then a darker possibility occurred to him. Maybe Nagy sold him out to the people he was after and that was the purpose of the stressful call that Fredric saw but could not hear at Nagy's office. In the end, he dismissed the thought that Nagy sent someone to trash the room to scare him. He wanted to trust his old friend.

Istvan observed, "You have got many bytes of data being transferred here. For sure, someone's using DSL to conduct video chats."

Fredric jumped to the edge of his chair once he saw that another phone call would be coming through. It was brief. "Is everyone in place in Washington and at the command center?" the voice asked.

"Yes."

"Excuse me a moment," Fredric told Istvan. Fredric immediately placed a telephone call to Walter Schneider.

"Since we are talking on a secure line, I have an update." Fredric relayed the conversation he had just heard about the financial trades.

Schneider paused for a moment and firmly said, "Whoever you were listening to is in the process of moving sizable sums of money. No telling why. Maybe they are moving some of the money they made from the operation they ran in Kenya. Or maybe they are trying to put money in places that might not raise any red flags from the authorities that track money laundering. Or maybe they are stashing money they are going to use for bribes. No telling, but you are clearly on to something. I find it interesting the references to the United States. But why...who knows."

Fredric responded, "At least there is nothing I have seen so far that would collaborate the intel that led us to think they were travelling to Berlin. I am no investment guru, but those trades sound pessimistic to me. It sounds like they are shorting the U.S. government."

"Financial crimes require significant more expertise than either you or I have. We do have whole teams who focus on this full-time, though," Schneider said. "Investors tend to overreact to any sort of negative economic news, so maybe there is a company on the American stock market that is about to announce that their sales fell far below the targets anyone expected, or maybe an accounting scandal is about to break. But I like your idea that maybe they are just trying to place the money in financial instruments that no one would expect."

Fredric thought this money could tie the people in the house he was monitoring to the Kenyan incident if the right people could trace the money.

"Very true," Fredric said aloud. "We need to break the encryption they are using and figure out what they are doing. Plus, these two phones from the people I eliminated will yield plenty more facts and ideas once we can break their password."

Schneider ignored the last statement, focusing on everything else he had heard. "I don't like the direction this is going. Maybe the U.S. is their next target. That wouldn't be good for us because the U.S. is a big trading partner of Germany. It will not help our economic interests if the type of chaos in Kenya spreads."

Fredric made sure his boss understood what he'd said. "You know I don't like to neutralize people, but two of their agents came for me and I had to take them down," he explained. "These people are dangerous. No telling what they are capable of."

"They really meant to kill you?" Schneider asked.

"One of them pulled out a gun, so yes, I think that is a safe assumption."

Schneider sounded like he didn't like this new development one bit. He continued, "I want you to get the phones back here so we can analyze them. We have to break the encrypted conversations you recorded. And we will coordinate with our counterparts who specialize in financial intelligence to begin unwinding those trades you heard. You are on to something and I think it is big, Fredric."

Fredric didn't hear praise from his boss very often, but he wasn't thinking so much of his pride as the ability to hunt down these cyber criminals. "Boss, we are dealing with a super-sophisticated enterprise. These people are incredibly well-connected and resourceful. I think they even have their tentacles inside the Hungarian government—and at the highest levels. We must do this in a way that Srepska doesn't know that we are after them. They know I am here, but they don't know where I am from or who I work for. The deeper and deeper we go, we need to be sure we stay a step ahead of them. This is my assignment. I want to keep following this lead, no matter where it takes me."

There was a pause on the phone. Then Schneider said, "You have a valid point. It seems from what you have been saying that the United States will be directly impacted by what these people are doing. I think we will work with the Americans on this. I don't want to get drawn into a joint operation, though. Srepska might retaliate against the German government if they find out we are helping the Americans go after them."

"That makes sense," Fredric replied.

Schneider quickly shuffled through his options. "I think we both now agree that we should not do the code-breaking, but there is a difference between handing the Americans raw intelligence that they have to make sense of and sharing analyzed intelligence with them. I can work out with the American Embassy there in Budapest for you to hand everything over so they can get it to our peers in the CIA or NSA. Then it is a simple handoff and we stay out of what happens next. The U.S. is easily advanced enough when it comes to combating cyber warfare."

Fredric didn't like that option. "Who knows if Srepska hasn't infiltrated someone into the American government so they can go around anything the Americans do? I want to make the handoff personally, to someone we trust."

"I have another idea," Schneider said, brightening with a new thought. "The new head of the American Justice Department was a classmate of mine some time ago when I was a foreign exchange student in the States, and we have stayed in contact after graduation. Perhaps I could reach out to him and see if he can help us. But I still demand that you get in and get out quickly. Our digital fingerprints cannot be associated with bringing them down." Fredric wasn't sure he liked this plan, but before he could respond, his boss added, "Let's talk again in two hours. Whether we go this route isn't a decision I can make by myself."

Fredric was doubtful about his plan. Telling some high-end official in the United States might well be the recipe for disaster. *But I can't miss this opportunity. I would be too embarrassed to ever face my superiors again if I said no.* Plus, he had to admit, he didn't want to get out of the game just yet. He was the one who had uncovered this nest of rats. He wanted to exterminate it too.

CHAPTER 8

SCHNEIDER PLACED A call and quickly worked through secure diplomatic channels to speak with the Attorney General. After initial disbelief by the American diplomatic staff, the message was conveyed to Jason Lim. "State just called and said that a Walter Schneider from the German government wants to talk to you," his secretary said flatly. "This guy says that it is absolutely urgent that he speak to you and you alone on a secure line. How shall I respond?"

"Walter Schneider?" Lim asked. That was a name he hadn't heard in a while, yet it stirred good memories. "Give me the number he wants me to call him on." Lim then dialed the number.

"The last time we spoke, you had quit your electrical engineering job and joined government service in Germany, if I recall right," Lim told Schneider.

"And you were thinking of going on to law school. You climbed fast, Jason, all the way to the top of the ladder."

"Woe is me. It is lonely at the top," Jason joked. "So, what's on your mind?"

Schneider recounted what Fredric had found. "We don't know for sure what they are doing. All we know is that your country seems to be on the radar screen of an extremely powerful criminal outfit that is proficient at cyber-crime. I cannot tell you what they have planned. But we think they're the same people who hacked a mobile phone company that has a financial services arm in Kenya, and we all saw how that destabilized the entire country. I don't know exactly what they are doing, though."

"It doesn't matter what they have planned," Jason said, concerned about the report. "If they are moving that sort of money around, that's a warning flag. I will be glad to serve as the liaison for you with the FBI," Lim said. "I need whatever evidence your agent has as quickly as possible so we can try to figure this out."

With that permission secured, Schneider called Fredric back. "It's a go," he said. "I have arranged for you to deliver the intel directly to the Attorney General. This will minimize the risk of the information being intercepted."

"The attorney general? Seriously? Isn't that going a few pay grades higher than you would normally go?"

Schneider fired back, "Yes. I will explain when you get back. Just remember, don't antagonize him. I mean it, don't mess this up. A lot is riding on you being my liaison."

Fredric hung up, thoroughly annoyed. "A messenger boy," he grumbled. "This is the thanks I get for breaking open a big case."

He pulled open his tablet computer and booked himself a flight that departed in five hours to Washington, DC. The flight would cost $8,000 since it was made so close to departure, but he would let the BND deal with that. He logged into a bank website and used a program to generate a credit card number specifically for the transaction.

"I am going to leave now," he told Istvan. "Keep recording. Stay here for an hour or so and then leave. Give me a big head start, okay?"

Fredric gathered his belongings and put them into his backpack. He disassembled his handgun, since when the hard-composite plastic parts were dispersed throughout the bag, it would never appear to be a gun when viewed on an x-ray machine at the airport. Even a hand-search would never identify it as suspicious.

"I am going to America. I may need your help once I get there if things don't go the way I expect."

Istvan was stunned by this development. "Wow, I have never been there."

"Don't worry, Istvan. If I need you, we will find a way to get you there. Until then, it has been great working with you." They shook hands and Istvan slapped him on the back.

Fredric put his legitimate German passport into his pocket. He put the passport that he used at the hotel, as well as the other passports he had with him, in an inner pocket of the bag, designed to look like the lining.

The two men had a toast. "To Wolfsburg winning the European Cup," Fredric said.

"No, to Újpesti winning," Istvan called after him.

Fredric left the hotel, and crossed the street when he saw a cab waiting at the corner. It was a silver Mercedes, with wide yellow markings on the sides. He took his backpack off, opened the door, and stepped inside. "To the airport," he told an unshaven young driver wearing a leather coat.

"Yes, of course."

The cab took off and soon approached an intersection where a sign marked the airport exit. It would have taken them onto Route 4, a busy highway. But the cab skipped the exit and kept going straight.

"Taking a different route than normal, are we?" Fredric commented.

"Yes, there is a big accident on the highway. I will get us to the airport by going a back way."

They drove another ten minutes. The cab passed traffic along the way, but it did not seem to be in any special hurry. Then the driver put on his turn signal and pulled off onto an exit.

"Just sit back and enjoy the ride."

Yet all Fredric saw were farms and fields in all directions. He saw a couple buildings that looked to be stores at one time, but had long since been abandoned. His antenna for trouble was tingling, and he glanced out the rear window. Two other cars behind him had gotten off the highway as well. What were the chances out in this rural area? Each car had two people in it. He knew what this meant. The people he was after had found him yet again. *How did that happen?* he wondered. Had they placed some kind of tracing device on anyone who monitored their phone calls?

"What do they grow out here?" Fredric asked with feigned curiosity. He wanted the driver to think he was still clueless.

"I really don't know," the cabbie said with a chuckle.

"How much longer until we get to the airport? I don't have a lot of time before my flight."

"This is the fastest route, trust me," the driver said coldly, without even looking in the rearview mirror at Fredric.

The car drove another half minute and then started slowing down.

"Oh no, the engine is losing power," the driver exclaimed. "I am sure that it is just the distributor wire. It tends to get loose and I have to push it back on more firmly. I am going to pull over here, stick it back in, and then we will be good to go."

Fredric immediately knew something was amiss. As a teenager, he had repaired cars and he knew that newer cars have electronic ignition systems. They didn't use distributor caps and wires. He breathed more rapidly, trying to assess his odds. Four people in the cars behind, plus the driver resulted in five against one, out in the middle of nowhere.

The taxi started pulling over to the side of the road. Fredric glanced behind and saw the same two cars behind him pull over too. He reached instinctively toward his ankle to retrieve his gun, but he caught himself before his hand reached very far. He remembered that he had disassembled it before going to the airport.

He opened the door and jumped out of the car after it came

to a near stop. There was nothing around to take cover from. How was he going to handle five against one? Quickly he bent down and scooped up some sand by the side of the road. That would do for starters.

The two cars following them had come to a stop a short distance back. Four men got out of the two cars and walked toward him.

The cabbie approached him from the opposite direction. Fredric knew the perils of allowing them to surround him. First things first, he thought grimly.

"Look, who is that over there?" Fredric lifted his hand to point. The driver, surprised that someone might be a witness, turned to look. Pivoting the upper half of his torso, Fredric released a devastating strike with his elbow. The tip slammed into the cabbie's temple, transferring the entire weight of Fredric's body into that one point.

The cabbie never knew what hit him. The only sound was the man's body hitting the ground with a thump. If he weren't dead, he'd be sleeping for a while.

Fredric turned toward the other four men approaching. He clenched his jaw. From the way they were coming straight at him, it looked like they had no training. They figured brute force and four-on-one odds would do the trick. *They are so much younger than I am,* he thought. Yet they would likely get into one another's way. *I have got to harness the fact that they won't be working in an effective synchronized partnership.*

He cautiously walked toward the four men, now ten feet away. One of them shouted out, "Hey, what was that about? We aren't going to hurt you, we just want to talk. We know what you did in the park, and yet we aren't here for revenge. If you help us, and tell us what we need to know, we will take you to the airport and all will be good. If you don't, we have ways to make your life miserable."

"Who do you work for?" Fredric asked.

"Don't play dumb with us, brother," another in the group yelled. "The boss gives us the orders, and we follow them."

"Just get in the car, tell us what we need, and you have a free pass to leave the country," the tallest in the group said.

Fredric thought back on the encounter in the park. There was zero likelihood that he would get out of there alive if he went along with their demands.

The fourth man was punching his fist into his hand in a menacing way as he said in a deep voice, "We are just here on orders of the boss. Nothing personal here."

He walked toward them calmly, saying: "Okay, you got a deal. You have got me outnumbered. I'll tell you everything you need to know, and I get to leave unharmed. It's a deal," he said calmly, while nodding his head and furrowing his brow. "Can we shake on it?"

In the next second, he tossed the sand in his hand in the eyes of the two men closest to him. They recoiled from the blast and started rubbing their eyes, cursing and stumbling around. That bought him just enough time to deal with the other two. The tall guy rushed toward him with his right fist cocked behind his head, as obvious as if he was shouting.

When the thug reached him, Fredric had no trouble sliding diagonally out of the line of the attack. The tall guy's fist passed by him and punched the air. Meanwhile, Fredric's knee rammed him in the gut. He boxed the man's ears hard. The man keeled forward, screaming in pain.

Fredric swiftly grabbed the guy's elbow from both sides and yanked it tightly against his chest. He pushed the attacker's elbow forward with his chest, which brought it to the point of breaking. Fredric's hands tightened, and the pain that rushed through the tall man's nervous system paralyzed him completely, rendered him helpless.

In the meantime, the fourth attacker found his way around his two buddies, and rushed furiously at Fredric with his arms opened wide. Fredric was still holding the tall man tightly as a shield. Wheeling, he released a sharp kick with the tip of his foot into the stomach of the onrushing man. His thumb hit a point just under his ribcage, and when he landed the strike, it caused the attacker's diaphragm to contract so strongly that it knocked all the air out of his lungs. He instantly fell to his knees, gasping and trying to catch his breath. Fredric delivered another kick, this time from the side, planting his heel in the thug's cheekbone. From the sharp crack that followed, Fredric knew that it would take him a couple of hours to regain consciousness.

By then the first two gangsters regained their eyesight, and once they realized what had happened during those couple of seconds they were out, they too rushed towards Fredric. One of them was clenching his fists, and the other one was reaching for his weapon.

Fredric swiftly turned the tall guy he was still holding firmly around, and he had to comply, since the searing pain from his elbow held at the breaking point was still preventing him from making any resistance. The first attacker slammed him in the head with his fist instead of Fredric and knocked him out. Just before the tall guy toppled to the dust, Fredric released his arm and shoved him toward the first attacker. The two bumped into each other, and while the first attacker was trying to avoid the collision, Fredric hit him with a hard uppercut at the tip of his chin.

The blow was not so hard, but it was very precise, and delivered just enough energy to disrupt his attacker and made him lose his balance. He fell down stunned, and tried to get back on his feet, but stumbled to the ground, as if he were drunk.

Fredric turned to the last thug, who was pulling out his gun. Fredric lashed out with a circular back sweep. Before the attacker could realize what was happening, his legs went flying up in the air, and his back and the back of his head slammed hard against the asphalt, causing him to drop his gun.

By this time, Fredric was sick and tired of this business. His knuckles were bruised, and he had a plane to catch. He picked up the gun that the gangster had dropped.

"Tell me who your boss is. Who is running your operation and how can I find him?" he asked. He was enraged at the man's lack of cooperation. He grabbed him by the hair and slammed his bloodied face against the pavement. The man was semi-conscious. "Serves you right," Fredric grumbled. The idiot probably didn't speak English anyway.

He lifted the gun, and first he shot out the front tires of the two cars parked behind the cab, and then he shot the back tires. He noticed a pair of long plastic handcuffs on the dashboard of the first car and some rope in the other one. He opened the door and grabbed the handcuffs quickly and then bound the hands of the other goons. He dragged them off the road and hurled them into a ditch, and then gathered all their car keys. Just to make sure he wasn't ambushed on the way to the airport.

He got in the cab, made a quick U-turn, and drove back through the farm-lined road back to the highway. He looked in his rearview mirror for any cars that might be after him. He checked his watch, and he still would be okay. Talk about building in travel time in case of any delays.

Soon the airport loomed up ahead. Its twin towers, almost resembling lighthouses, seemed to welcome him. Phase two had begun.

CHAPTER 9

BACK AT THE hotel, Istvan had shut the computer down and was reaching for his bag when he heard a knock on the door. "Room service," came the voice from the other side. He looked through the peephole and saw someone holding a stainless-steel cover for a food tray. He was puzzled. He hadn't called for room service. Nor had Fredric, as far as he knew. The person knocked again. Then again, he thought, perhaps Fredric had placed an order on his way out as a going-away present.

As he opened the door, the waiter said with a louder than expected voice, "I have the meal you ordered."

Istvan glanced down and saw the man had a gun in his right hand as he was balancing the food tray with his left.

"Get inside," he said under his breath as he lurched forward.

Istvan felt the blood drain from his face. *I never expected this.* He wished that Fredric was still there. Surely, his partner would have an answer to this. He began backing up into the room.

The man quickly shut the door. He put the food tray down on the bed, setting the stainless-steel cover to clattering, while keeping the gun pointed at Istvan. The man scanned the room and looked to see if anyone was in the bathroom, turning the light on in the process. "Sit down," he shouted to Istvan while pointing to the chair in front of the table where Istvan's computer sat.

When the intruder was finished with checking the place, he asked, "What are you doing here?"

Istvan was unsure of what to say. "I was hired to help someone here with a project. I was just getting ready to leave." He was thinking that perhaps he could talk his way out of the situation. How would this gunman know what he was doing?

"I am looking for the guy you were working with. What type of project were you doing for him?" the man asked.

"He just needed some computer consulting services. Needed some help debugging some software code," Istvan added, trying to add some convincing specifics. "He was in a rush and needed to catch a train, and I was just getting ready to leave. I don't know anything else."

"That's not really what you were doing. Tell me again, what were you doing for him?" the man said while waving his gun.

He kept piling on excuses, hoping to establish his innocence. "I am just a computer consultant. I don't even know who I was working for. I just got a call to help someone, I never got his name or contact information, and now he is gone."

"How do I find this person you were helping? If he went to the train station, where is he going?"

"He didn't say. I really don't know. I don't know his phone number, email, or anything." Istvan realized that sounded weak, and to make up for it, he offered, "But if we go to the train station now, I will point him out to you. How about that? I point him out."

"No way. What's going on over there?" he asked while pointing to the computers.

"Those aren't mine," Istvan said. His hands were trembling.

"For some reason, I don't think so."

"I really don't know much," Istvan said. "How about we go to the train station and I lead you to him? His train could be departing soon, so if you really are after him and not just trying to rob me, we would need to leave now."

"I am not here to rob you. I don't need your crappy computers. I have two buddies who are dead, and I think you know who killed them and why. I am not leaving here until you tell me."

"Really, I don't know who this guy was. He didn't want to tell me anything about his background."

"Was he Hungarian?"

Istvan paused. Maybe the intruder didn't know very much beyond whatever this killing business was about. "I communicated with him in English. I think he was from South Africa," Istvan said. "He definitely was not from around here. He never told me who he worked for. I wish I could help you."

Istvan glanced at the gun, then at the door. If only Fredric were here, Istvan thought desperately. Fredric would know how to get out of this.

"I think you are going to come with me," the man said. "Pack up the computer. You are going to walk out with me. If you do anything to draw attention to us or yell for help, I will shoot you immediately. Is that understood?" he asked.

"Yes," Istvan sheepishly said.

"Well, get your stuff packed up. It's time to go," he said while glancing around the room.

Soon Istvan had everything ready to go. "Can I put my jacket on?" he asked.

"Yes. As we go out, I am going to put my gun in my coat pocket, but remember, I will use it. We will get in a car that will be waiting outside."

Using his phone, the man sent a text message. Istvan was amazed at how he seemed to be texting while keeping his aim and gun pointed at him.

"Let's go."

Istvan walked to the door, feeling like he was walking a mile.

He continued to wonder what he should do. As he opened the door, he turned around suddenly and tried to grab the gun from the man. Istvan didn't know what he was doing, he was just acting on impulse.

For his clumsy effort, Istvan was rewarded by the man whacking him with the gun. He clenched his jaw with his hands in extreme pain, then realized he needed to fight back. Istvan launched a wild punch. The intruder leaned away, easily avoiding the swing. Istvan lunged forward for a second try. The man pulled the trigger on the gun.

Istvan froze at the muffled retort. Blood was coming out of his chest. The man pulled the trigger again with another muffled *thump*. Istvan slumped to the floor in pain. The man grabbed Istvan's bag and quickly left the room.

He walked to the stairwell calmly. He passed through the lobby and got into a car waiting around the corner from the front door. The driver pulled away quickly as the man opened Istvan's bag.

"Where's the kid?" the driver asked. "You were supposed to grab the kid."

"Punk tried to jump me, so I had to shoot him. The kid was a *bolond*," he said, fretting. "At least this computer will help us figure out who they are and what they are up to."

"You better hope so," the driver snarled. "Or Zoltan will use that stupid gun on you."

CHAPTER 10

LARS CHRISTOPHERSON WAS on a seven-mile run. Not just any run, but nearly half a mile on a trail barely three feet wide through a small forested area before beginning the ascent of a five-thousand-foot mountain outside Pasadena, in the San Gabriel range. He didn't have a water bottle because he liked the independence of not having to carry anything. And he didn't carry a camelback because he didn't like to have to occasionally clean it. Rather, for this run, he counted on a water fountain located conveniently about his halfway point near the forest office. Often, it worked.

He was considering whether he should register for an upcoming half-marathon. When he was younger, he didn't like to run, but he had slowly warmed to it. Now it was his favorite outdoor activity—at least, when he had interesting scenery and a course where he never crossed the same point more than twice. He ran as much to stay in shape as to challenge himself and clear his mind.

Once he finished his run, he began walking increasingly slower to cool down and slow down his heartrate. He was annoyed as he reached his car and noticed that another car had parked so close that he had to avoid bumping it as he opened the door. He scanned all the empty spaces around the nearby Rose Bowl and wondered why the moron couldn't have chosen any other space.

Opening the trunk of his car, he got out a bottle of water and drank it as he did his stretching exercises in front of his car. He checked his watch and was annoyed that he hadn't run at a faster pace. Then again, he had passed almost everyone else on the trail.

As he finished stretching, he was looking forward to going to the local Jamba Juice to have a cold fruit smoothie and recharge for the rest of his day. He got in the car and drove south, toward downtown Pasadena. His lean face, framed by wavy blonde hair, was still red from the workout. His polarized, partially rimless Oakley sunglasses covered his green eyes as Haydn's Surprise symphony played on KUSC, a local public radio station.

His phone rang. He looked down on the phone, and the caller ID indicated that the number of the person calling him was blocked. He pulled over and parked in front of a driveway on a quiet, tree-lined street. He had not yet configured the hands-free call feature of his phone so that he could legally talk while driving.

"I got your number from the Milan Factor," the caller said with a heavy German accent.

He took a deep breath. He knew this was a code word indicating that the caller had been in touch with a confidant who had for years been a reliable source of referrals.

"Okay, I am listening, what do you need?"

"My name is Walt, and I work for a European nation's intelligence service. I heard that you are very good at what you do, and that you have a lot of expertise in undercover operations. You come highly recommended. I need to hire you for a job. We will pay you $250,000. As I am sure you know, you are on your own. If anyone asks, we never hired you, we never talked, and of course you never heard of us. Interested in learning more?"

"Those terms can work quite nicely, but what exactly do you need taken care of? And when? What are we talking about?"

"Srepska. They—"

Lars immediately interjected, since he made it his business to know things. "You mean the financial crime syndicate that no one knows what to do anything about?"

"You got it. We just received raw intelligence that they are running money through a small bank in Los Angeles. Based on the large dollar amount of the transactions, the bank must be aware of the scheme. We want to confirm this is true. And if it is, we want to know as much as we can about their dealings with Srepska. We want to know who their past targets have been, who runs them, everything you can. The money transfers should be a valuable lead for you."

Lars was interested, but he had a question. "And you called me? Why didn't you call the FBI?"

"There is a good reason. Despite the information my people just found, there may or may not be an inside connection between Srepska and the United States. I don't have enough trust in the FBI to ask them to conduct an investigation. You have ways to get information that won't compromise our efforts."

Lars asked, "So, what are you saying, exactly? You want me to work up a case and then hand it off to the FBI? I don't see that happening. They'll just arrest me. And that's not how I work."

"No," Schneider said. "We want you to expose the ringleaders of Srepska. If you are so inclined, we will hire you to take them out. Or you might find that our lead doesn't amount to anything. In that case, your job would be done quickly."

Lars took some time to consider the offer. He knew the lead was legitimate and also felt strongly that the caller was withholding information that he would like to know. He wasn't sure if the man was being truthful about his reasons for not going to the FBI.

"Are you still there?" Schneider asked.

Lars replied quickly. "That is a big challenge. I don't take jobs unless I can do what my client wants. Give me something more to go on here if you want me to do this."

"I tell you, we have a very strong lead. Germany has a consulate office in Los Angeles. Tell them you are there to see the attaché for economic trade. You will get the information you need to explore whether Srepska has a California connection."

If he was going to a foreign consulate office, this meant the project he was about to undertake was sanctioned by at least some part of the German government. *Having a country for a client is problematic,* Lars thought as he wondered what he could get drawn into. *But then again, this is not a case involving another country. It is targeting a criminal outfit that every country is after,* Lars thought.

"What you want me to do is risky. Complex. Time consuming. As I just said, I have a reputation to uphold and I don't take a job unless I know I will succeed. You have to give me more hard information to go on. And…I won't take the job for less than $400,000. Fifty percent paid up front. Fifty percent paid within seven days of when the job is done. I get paid in cash or gold. I don't start work until I am paid."

"Okay, it is a deal," the man said hastily. "The money and the information we have will be waiting for you. What name do you want me to tell them will be picking it up?"

Lars glanced at the newspaper on his passenger's side seat and made up a name based on two names he saw. "Tell them it will be Franklin Noonan."

After Lars hung up, he was pleased. He suddenly had new afternoon plans—but only after his lunchtime treat to himself. He resumed his drive to get his smoothie. He soon saw the familiar sign and parked at the head of the street. About two-thirds of his car was parked along a curb painted red, but he'd just have to take the chance.

He walked in and soon his order was ready. But as Lars tried to use his MasterCard debit card to pay, the transaction was declined. Lars was perplexed. He had checked his bank account just the day before and there was plenty of money in the account. Then he realized he wasn't alone. The next guy in line couldn't pay with his MasterCard either.

Someone in line shouted, "I had the same problem at the drugstore across the street."

But the person behind Lars in line could pay with a VISA card. "Come on, I mean, what's wrong? Why won't my Master-Card work but only a VISA will?" he grumbled.

But Lars had no VISA card on him, or any cash. He was frustrated, but he dismissed the issue. He was focused on getting started on his new assignment. *A smoothie is not what I am getting paid to worry about*, he thought.

He went home and showered. He changed into a pair of black Dockers and a yellow Polo shirt. He drove across town to the German consulate office.

He walked in and announced confidently, "I am here to see the attaché for economic trade regarding the Milan project."

"I am not sure we have anyone with that title here," the receptionist asked. "What is this concerning?"

Lars was taken aback. *Was that call I received genuine?* Maybe someone was pulling a prank on him. "The attaché is expecting me to discuss an important matter that your colleagues in Germany wanted me to come here to discuss."

"Well, that doesn't help me much. What is your name?" she asked.

Lars appeared indignant. "My name is Franklin Noonan."

Just then another receptionist came back. "Are you Franklin?" she asked.

"Yes," Lars said with a whiff of anger in his voice.

"My apologies, I had to step away for a moment. Follow me and I will take you to him," she said, opening the door to let him back into their offices.

He went in empty-handed and left with a briefcase filled with $100 bills. *That's enough to pay for a few smoothies.* He also had tucked in his pocket a flash drive that he was told had the information to get him started.

Inside his car, he pulled a Surface ultra-slim laptop computer from the case under his seat and plugged in the flash drive. So, let's just see what our local bankers are up to, he thought. What new ways have they devised to break the law?

CHAPTER 11

AFTER FREDRIC LANDED at Dulles Airport in suburban Washington, he began to plot out how he'd go about this assignment. After nearly being killed in Budapest, he had no guarantee that whoever had the skill to track him down to his second hotel hadn't followed him overseas. He was leery of using a taxi, rental car, or public transportation.

Fredric looked out the hotel window, reflecting on how the night before, he had caught a bus out of Dulles airport and got on and off Metro light rail trains until he was convinced that no one was following him and circled back to the airport.

Outside, he spotted a bicycle trail. Even better, nearby was a bicycle shop with new and used bikes for sale. He had a bicycle jersey and shorts in his backpack. D.C. was a lot warmer than Germany or Hungary. And it didn't take much to persuade him to use a bike to get into the city. *Maybe I'll see what they have to offer.*

Fredric walked over to the bike shop. He scanned the bikes. Unlike bike shops he was used to, the bikes represented practically every manufacturer of bikes large and small – and there was no apparent order to the layout of the bikes.

"Do you have a 62 centimeter here?" he asked referring to the frame size.

"This is the closet we have got," the clerk said. "It's a 19 inch. We don't carry anything bigger."

He purchased a used bike for $300 cash. It was much heavier than the feather-light bikes he normally rode, but at least it looked sturdy. *If I get knocked to the ground on the bike, I won't have to worry about the frame breaking.*

Outside the shop, rolling his new bicycle along, he read a sign that told him the bikeway was a former railway line that had been converted into a sixty-mile bicycle trail. Portions of the trail went through suburban neighborhoods, while others wove between farm fields. He watched several people who sped by on their bikes wearing backpacks, and he contemplated whether they might be bicyclists commuting to work. He noticed others who were wearing fitness gear, clearly using the trail for recreation. He glanced at a sign that warned cyclists to yield to runners, who were supposed to yield to walkers. *I can do that. This trail is so much wider, straight, and truly built to accommodate cyclists and runners,* he thought. The urban paths in Munich were too crowded and narrow for him to ride on…at least ride on at the speed he wanted.

He took off for an early ride, before the bureaucrats lumbered into their offices. *Likely with a bag of donuts,* Fredric thought cheerfully, enjoying the clear country air. He came upon a clearing alongside the trail about twenty-five miles from downtown DC that featured three picnic benches under a small open-air building. At least ten bikes could be parked on the nearby bike racks, and he realized it was a popular break point. Curiously, it was known as Jones' Switch Station, he discovered from a sign, because of how the location was used for nearly eighty years when the trail was a railway line.

Passing a man wearing black bicycle shorts and a bicycle jersey emblazoned with a big beer bottle and the logo *Warsteiner,* Fredric filled his water bottle, as it was empty after forty-five minutes of biking. Walking over to the picnic bench, he reached into the black backpack he'd set on the table and retrieved the phone. He stepped back a few feet to be farther away from the trail but still well within eyesight of his bicycle. He glanced around and was for the first time of the day completely comfortable no one was tailing him.

"This is Fredric. I just left the hotel. Is the coast clear?" he said in a soft voice, speaking English with a nearly undetectable German accent. No bystanders were around to hear the sharp contrast in his tone of speech, given his imposing stature.

"Yes. They are waiting on you," the voice on the other end of the phone answered. "Remember, you are to just drop it off and then leave and return here immediately."

"I understand. I will arrive at the destination shortly."

Fredric put the phone back in his bag and lifted the straps of the backpack around his back. Before he started off, he reached into the unzipped pocket of his bag and retrieved a Mint Chocolate Clif Energy Bar. He quickly ate it and tossed the wrapper in the trash can.

The GPS app on his phone told him that at an average speed of twenty miles per hour, the trip would take little more than an hour. *That won't be any problem.* He set off at his usual pace, enjoying the passing scenery. About five miles outside downtown DC, he faced a choice: whether to go straight on Four Mile Run Trail, or turn left to take Custis Trail. He stopped to check his phone and it showed that either route would get him to his destination. Then two cyclists, both female, zipped by him, going straight. They were on bicycles built for speed—much akin to Fredric's bike back in Germany—whereas Fredric's recently purchased used bicycle was old, relatively slow, and a tad too small for Fredric's frame.

No matter, he thought. Using his endurance training, he biked fast to catch up to them. He pulled even with them on a hill in another half mile. He remarked, "Nice day this time of year for a ride," as he passed. They took an exit off the bike trail, while Fredric continued straight into the heart of the city.

He soon went down a slight hill, under a dark bridge, around a corner, and up another hill. Exploring a new city was getting to be fun, and he had to remind himself he wasn't here for pleasure. He soon approached another path, one called the Mount Vernon trail. He saw a sign indicating that Georgetown was to his right. He went in that direction, passing several other cyclists along the way.

He glanced ahead and saw a line of monuments across the river. Just as he was wondering if it would be easy for him to cross the river on his bicycle, he saw a trail going up over a long bridge that ended in front of the Jefferson Memorial. *Now, this is more like it.* He biked around the memorial and Tidal Basin and soon saw the Washington Monument off in the distance. He looked at his phone, and the directions on the mapping app directed him to keep going straight. As he biked in front of the Lincoln Memorial, he stared up at it but didn't slow down. He reached Independence Avenue and noticed the White House off in the distance.

He kept heading downtown until he noticed a bike lane in the center of Constitution Avenue. He soon drove by two men and three women in front of a National Capital Peoples Bank ATM. They were angrily pointing at the ATM with their debit cards in hand. He noticed several blocks away a bank employee hanging a sign that said "Out of service for repairs" in front of a Mega National Bank ATM. Teachers and Parents Federal Credit Union also had a few people with quizzical looks on their faces as the branch was closed on a weekday. He was puzzled by this systemic breakdown right in the capital of the United States. *It certainly isn't German precision. Then again,* he thought, *this isn't Germany,* as he glanced with disgust at the overflowing trash receptacles.

He soon reached a grandiose building on Constitution Avenue blocks from the White House. Life-sized perched eagles made from limestone on the building's exterior combined with the leviathan doors projected a sober yet distinguished appearance. He noticed the sign out front: Robert F. Kennedy U.S. Justice Building. He biked around three sides of it until he saw a narrower street with a bike rack where three bikes were secured. He had no lock, so he used a twig on the ground to lift the chain off the crank. The chain sagged to the ground. The odds of the old bike still being there when he returned, despite the bike not being locked up, had suddenly improved because someone couldn't just walk up and ride it off without having some technical know-how on what to do.

At the front door, all four guards in the entryway turned their attention to the stocky man wearing cycling gear and a backpack. They all stared quizzically, but suspected he was just another bike messenger with a delivery. As he approached the guards, he said, "I am Walter Smith, and I have an appointment to see Jason Lim."

A pudgy middle-aged guard sitting down behind the security desk jumped up. He motioned toward Fredric and remarked, "Follow me, please. Just walk through the metal detector." He put his bag through an x-ray machine as another guard inspected in a disinterested way. "You are good to go," he said, utterly bored.

The guard who had first greeted him led him to an elevator. "I was told to expect you, sir. I will take you to Mr. Lim's. You must be a big cyclist," he said, pointing at the gear. "I bought a bike a couple years ago and keep meaning to ride it to get some exercise, but I haven't gotten around to it."

Fredric had heard excuses like this before. "I don't bike for exercise. I do it to push myself. That's what you have to do for road races and time trials."

"Whoa. I don't think I'll be getting to that anytime soon."

Now Fredric felt badly. "Don't let me talk you out of it. Riding is the best feeling in the world."

The elevator soon took them to the top floor. Fredric felt out of place as all the buttoned-down people in the hallways stared at his unconventional attire.

He was quickly taken into a large office with a magnificent view of the Capitol. "I'm Jason Lim. Can I offer you anything?"

asked a well-dressed, fit man said as he rose from behind a solid oak table. "I bet you could use a glass of water."

Fredric scanned the office. Déjà vu, he thought, given he had been in a similar setting in Budapest a few days earlier. He only hoped he wouldn't be sold out this time.

"No, thank you," Fredric said. He didn't have any interest in exchanging pleasantries, so he got right to the point. "It is extremely important that your people get started right away on processing the information that I have. I have internet addresses for computers being used by Srepska—you know who they are, right?"

The attorney general looked stunned at Fredric's directness. "Yes, Walter filled me in."

"Okay, I have those, plus I have phones belonging to a couple of their operatives, logs of their internet traffic, some recordings of their calls, and some instructions on how to access more. They are moving large sums of money around, and I doubt that it is being used for legal purposes. I don't know what sort of scam they have going. They know I am on their trail, so you need to get busy with this information fast before they try to cover their tracks."

"Yes, sir. I'll have our top people get right on this. Thank you for your service. And thank you for coming halfway around the world to deliver this," Lim said as he motioned to the sofa in his office.

"It is important that I get going. My job is simply to deliver these materials. That's all I am authorized to do. But first, who knows that I am here?" Fredric asked.

Lim answered, "You don't need to worry. Everyone who works in this building must undergo a background check. Nothing to worry about at all." He flinched under Fredric's unrelenting stare. "Let's see, my secretary knew you were coming, as does a deputy director at the FBI. And the law student who is interning for me knows—in fact, if she were here, you could thank her for getting you waived through security and up to my office so quickly."

Fredric didn't feel any of Lim's confidence. He would have preferred that only Lim knew. He wondered if his boss had made that clear. "I would feel a lot more comfortable if no one other than those who are essential to this mission knew."

Fredric listened to Lim innocently recount how he had informed key staff in his department that he was about to get a package involving national security from a German operative. Fredric groaned, knowing that a Srepska agent could be monitoring Lim's emails. After all, his visit to his old friend Nagy had put him in the sights of Srepska to begin with.

Fredric had to nail down exactly what was known about him. Lim seemed welcoming and earnest. Everything seemed eerily quiet in the room—no sounds of other people talking, printers running, or phones ringing. He heard the sound of blowing air coming through the vents, but nothing else.

"Did you tell them exactly why I was here?" Fredric asked.

"Yes."

"Using the phrase Srepska," Fredric asked with a concerned look.

"Yes."

There was nothing to be done about it now. Fredric passed over the materials. Lim then asked Fredric how he could be reached if needed. While asking the question, Lim handed Fredric a notepad and pen.

Fredric wrote out the number for the prepaid cellphone that he had earlier purchased at the airport. Lim pulled out his Blackberry and typed the number in as Fredric was writing.

Lim then bid Fredric farewell. "I should get to work now. I wish you a safe journey back. But can I get someone to take you to the airport? That's the least I can do."

Fredric did not feel comfortable getting into a car, not after

Hungary. "No, thanks. I have a long flight ahead of me, and there is nothing like stretching my muscles with a bike ride to the airport. I have a flight tonight back to Germany."

"It's your call," Lim said cheerfully. He cocked a finger at Fredric and smiled. "Tell my old buddy Walter that the next pepperoni pizza is on me. You need help getting back down?"

"No, I can find my way."

The two shook hands, and Fredric left Lim in his office. Yet he deliberately left the door open. After what he had recently experienced, he wanted to make sure this American was on the level. Lim's secretary was away from her desk, so Fredric retreated just enough so that the door hid him from sight.

Lim did not pick up the phone. But only a few seconds passed before a side door opened. Fredric had hardly noticed it, given how large and opulent the office was. A beautiful young woman entered, looking like she was all business. "Good job," she said. "You continue to keep your end of the bargain, and I will keep ours."

What the hell did that mean?

Yet Fredric did not have a chance to find out more. The secretary reentered the outer office, and seeing Fredric snooping, she marched right toward him and firmly closed the door. "Can I help you further?"

You meddling old... "No, I had just remembered something on my way out."

Fredric navigated the maze-like hallways of the building and took the elevator back down. His bike was exactly where he left it. With the help of a twig and a plastic grocery bag over his hand to protect it from getting greasy, the bike that at first looked to be broken down suddenly was ready to take Fredric on the next leg of his journey.

He wasn't taking the night flight back to Germany, though. He would hole up instead, calling his boss to tell him that something suspicious was going on. He was going to petition to stay on further.

He mounted the bicycle and started off toward the street. Walter must know other people in Washington, people who could access information Fredric needed. Because he was positive that Srepska was not running the largest heist in history from some rundown dump in Budapest.

CHAPTER 12

WALKING IN THROUGH the side door of the attorney general's office was a brunette woman in her late twenties, wearing a dark short skirt suit. What Fredric did not see was that she had a Department of Justice identification card around her neck. She proceeded to sit on the couch in the attorney general's office, holding a tablet computer. Lim had the materials that Fredric brought on his desk, and he was in the process of starting to examine them.

"Good job. You continue to keep your end of the bargain, and I will keep ours," she said with a smirk.

Lim looked up, startled. "Excuse me? What are you talking about, Natasha? What bargain? I am busy right now, so I don't have time to talk with you. I have a very sensitive problem to deal with. Come back at the end of the day and we can see if I am free then."

He looked back down, with an annoyed look on his face. He reached for the phone and started to dial a number.

"No, Jason, we are going to deal with this right now. Remember the loan from Indiana? Remember what else we did to help you at the same time? Well everyone will know the full story about your drug company unless you hand everything over. If you give me what that guy just brought you, the loan will be forgiven and no one will ever know about the money you borrowed and under what circumstances." Lim looked at her in alarm, his hands moving to protect the documents Fredric had given him. Her eyes turned steely as she went on. "You made a promise when you borrowed the money that you would repay it. The loan is due now. Payable in full by turning over what you were just given."

Lim slammed the phone receiver down. "Excuse me?" he said in an indignant tone.

"You heard me. The loan you took out in return for that German spy's information."

He had hoped this day would never come. And at such a cost. He was betraying an old friend of his. He might be betraying his country during a severe crisis, if what Fredric had said was true. Yet they had him over a barrel. Now that he had attained the position of attorney general, he could not bear to be disgraced. His career would be over.

Several silent moments elapsed.

Then, Lim reluctantly tossed the USB drive that Fredric had brought him. His intern, Natasha, reached down to pick it up.

"You have made a wise decision, believe me. These people would not hesitate to kill you to get what they want." She tucked the flash drive into a pocket of her jacket. "Oh, and there is one other favor we have to ask."

"What else do you want?" Lim asked with a heavy voice.

She continued, "It is very simple and won't cost you a penny. Won't hurt your reputation at all. What I need you to do is completely risk-free. Here it is: when the President calls you to a meeting and announces that he found out who is waging electronic warfare on the U.S., I want you to support what he says and say your investigative staff just uncovered documentation of what he says happened. And of course, you will tell anyone who knew he was coming and is expecting to receive what he sent over that the flash drive was corrupted."

Lim was confused. "What do you mean? How can I say I will do something that I don't even know what that is? If I get asked

a question, I won't know the answer and I will look like a fool."
"Trust the President. Trust his judgment and simply agree that he
is correct. After all, you helped him get elected and he appointed
you to this job, so you really aren't going to doubt him, are you?"

Lim was very unhappy. "It still doesn't make a lot of sense to
me. Maybe I just walk away from what you are trying to have me
do. After all, I took an oath to uphold the laws of the United States
and the Constitution."

But Natasha fired back, "It is non-negotiable. Just do this one
little thing for us, support your President, and all will be over. If
you don't, your career and life as you know it will be in the toilet."

Lim had an equally quick response. "You will never get away
with this. You cannot blackmail the attorney general like this. You
must be really naive."

She then took out a phone. "Okay, so you don't want to
take the deal. Do you mind if I make a call?" She started to dial
a number.

At last Lim capitulated. "Fine, you get your way." He turned
his back to her and his desk, on which all of the materials that
Fredric had earlier brought sat.

She advanced to the desk and swept all of the material into her
pockets. She swiftly left Lim's office carrying the phones and other
media that Fredric had handed to Lim.

Once alone in the conference room, she made a call. "We have
it all. And Lim is ours. Threat diverted," she said. "The spy? He
left. No, I don't know where he is."

Back in his palatial office, Lim took his glasses off and rubbed
his forehead. He then stared out the window before his chief deputy came into his office. "So, here's the latest update on the Rich-
mond scandal." She filled him in on the steps that had been taken.
They agreed that the problem was probably not a criminal matter
under the responsibility of the Justice Department to investigate.

The Chief Deputy then asked about Fredric.

Lim tried not to gulp audibly. "He actually didn't have anything of any substance to share. It was a hoax. Forget about him, we need to stay focused."

After the Chief Deputy left his office, Lim told his secretary to clear his calendar for the rest of the day and to tell anyone who tried to reach him that he was unavailable. He was going to figure how to make this situation right.

CHAPTER 13

LARS HAD STARTED the day at the ungodly hour of eight o'clock. How all the worker bees actually got up in the morning and arrived at work by that time was a secret he never wanted to learn. As Los Angeles traffic eased down from the morning rush hour, he drove from his house in Pasadena to downtown Los Angeles.

Lars knew all the local highways and byways. Although he was born in Stockholm, as in Sweden, he had lived in the greater Los Angeles area since he was two years old. He and his parents moved to Los Angeles for a chance of a new life, but unlike their plans, they spent Lars's entire childhood in a working-class neighborhood in the Inland Empire east of the city. Thanks to their sacrifices, he became successful—educationally and later financially.

Unlike the day before, when ATM failures were scattered, by now the problems had become severe. An all-news station was playing on the radio, and the newscaster reported that ATM machines were out of service all over the city. Large retailers and other merchants that would normally accept checks refused to do so because the verification software they used at the point of sale terminal could not validate that the checks were valid. Plus, many bank tellers were unable to determine how much money were in customers' accounts because of payment system problems that were starting to impact other bank systems. Employers were discussing how they would make payroll given that the systems through which money would temporarily flow between banks was down.

At least one bank branch had closed its doors, according to a reporter who was visiting bank branches in West Los Angeles. It had a sign on its door that said, "Closed because of electrical problems." A random person interviewed by the reporters noted, "I need my money now. You know, they can't just decide they won't open up today."

Once in downtown Los Angeles, Lars exited off the freeway and pulled into the underground parking lot of a tall office building. He drove down two floors in the garage, circling around until he found a parking space near the elevator.

He took a marble-lined car up to the main floor. Seeing a sign that all visitors needed to check in, he went to the security guard desk and took out from his jacket pocket a thin wallet that displayed a badge. "I am an investigator from the State of California Franchise Tax Board here to visit CityFargo Bank," he said. He produced his badge and flashed an ID card. The alarmed guard typed his name into the computer, quickly printed him an ID sticker for the building, and gave him a card to get through the turnstile and onto the elevator.

Lars passed through the turnstile and onto the elevator to the thirty-sixth floor. He walked into the corporate offices of CityFargo, a bank that had twenty branches throughout Southern California. It had a reputation as a customer-oriented bank for small businesses. Analysts considered the bank to be small but profitable. As this wasn't a retail branch but instead the bank's corporate office, it was still open despite the fact that its branches, like those of its competitors, were unable to help consumers complete most transactions.

Outfitted in a tailored solid black suit and starched white shirt with blue tie, he flashed a badge to reception personnel within the bank. "I am an investigator and I have a warrant," he said. "Point me toward the office of your CEO." The young lady at the front desk froze initially, before jumping up and saying, "Follow me."

While they were walking down a hallway, he said, "This relates to a very confidential matter that is being investigated under seal, so under no circumstances are you to mention or relay the existence of my warrant or this investigation to anyone."

She shook her head as she nonchalantly said, "Okay. What was your name again?" she asked.

She opened the door to the CEO's suite. "You have a Mr. Jameson here to see you."

Lars slipped past her and closed the door. He then turned the lock for privacy. What was about to happen in the office wasn't meant for prying eyes.

Lars took a moment to look out the window over the greater Los Angeles landscape. He observed the blue ocean on one side, and the mountains, hidden in smog, on the other. The office was serenely quiet, although it was the size of a small studio apartment.

The CEO, Marvin Pierce, showed an expression that matched the words out of his mouth, "Who are you?"

Lars wasn't going to be intimidated by a know-it-all banker. "How much are they paying you?" he fired back.

"Excuse me?" Pierce said.

"You heard me, how much money are you getting for this?"

"I don't know what you are talking about. Get out of my office now," the CEO said in a loud voice.

He reached for his phone, but found it was dead. Lars had already taken that precaution. He took out a small electronic scrambler in his shirt pocket. He held it up and flashed a wide grin as the CEO stared quizzically at it.

Lars took out of his leather shoulder bag a tablet computer. He quickly typed in a password, and within a few seconds, he turned the tablet computer around and showed it to the CEO.

A look of horror suddenly appeared on his face.

Pierce slammed back down in his seat. The flash drive in the package that Lars had retrieved with his payment had provided him with some crucial pieces of evidence—proof of money transfers that involved entities on a list of individuals and organizations who were prohibited by the Treasury Department from holding bank accounts in the U.S. The mere fact that Pierce recognized the names told Lars that the CEO was not an innocent bystander of their illegal transactions. He was definitely on the right path.

"I am not going to ask again," Lars demanded. "Why are you letting your bank do business with an international crime syndicate? Don't just tell me it's for the money. Tell me how you first got involved with these people."

The CEO, though, recovered from his initial shock. In a futile gesture, he tossed a book on his desk toward Lars. He easily leaned his head out of the way.

"I'm starting to get annoyed," Lars said. He reached into his bag and pulled out a small black firearm with a long tip. It was a favorite weapon of his, a M&P22 pistol with a suppressor along with supersonic/subsonic ammo. "Why don't we use this instead?"

The CEO gasped at the gun aimed at his face.

Lars said, "You are coming with me."

The CEO, trying to take charge of the situation, firmly said, "Who sent you?"

As Lars clicked off the safety on his black semi-automatic handgun, the CEO seemed to realize that cooperation would be his best strategy.

Lars motioned to the door. "We are leaving now, fatso. Get up and walk out the door to the elevator. You will tell your secretary that you are going with me to have a cup of coffee and that you may end up going down to Santa Monica to check out a big potential loan opportunity afterward. If you don't cooperate, I will shoot you. Do you understand me? I will leave your brains splattered all over your nice white carpet. And, if for some reason something were to happen unexpectedly, my partner knows that you live on 2322 Yates Street, and he knows how and where and when to find your wife Shana and your child Tustin. Don't play any games with me."

The CEO sat stunned for several seconds.

In the background in Pierce's office, Lars quickly glanced at CNN. The cameras showed a neighborhood in Chicago where people were hurrying out of two small independent businesses next door to each other. Looting was already erupting in major cities. The headline on the screen appeared, "Across America, fear and uncertainty reigns in the streets."

Lars recalled what happened when he went to buy a smoothie. What he saw on television must be connected to the job he had. *Could I have been hired to try to prevent what was happening, just hired too late?* He then said, "Let's go now," as he put his hand with the gun into his pocket. "Do you see that little bulge?" he asked the banker. "That little bulge will kill you. Now, let's go."

As Lars instructed, the CEO told his secretary that he would be leaving for a little while, and they walked to the elevator.

As the door opened, Lars remarked, "You do what I tell you to, and you will be fine. You try to become a hero, and I'll leave your blood all over the marble in your elevator."

Lars and the CEO got in the elevator and soon they were down in the parking garage. "Follow me," he said.

They walked toward a blue Mini Cooper parked near the elevator bank. Lars reached into his back pocket and pulled out a pair of handcuffs. "Put these on. Because I'm such a good guy, I'll let you keep your hands in front, not behind your back," he told the CEO. Pierce held the handcuffs, not sure how to work them. Lars roughly grabbed his hands and snapped the handcuffs on. "You bankers really are worthless, aren't you? Only good for stealing people's hard-earned money." Lars then opened the passenger side door of his car. "Get in, fatty."

Lars was walking around to the driver's side when he noticed that the attendant in the parking garage had seen everything. Lars took out the badge from his wallet and waved it at him. He shouted, "Official police business."

The valet quickly looked down and away as if he had no interest in someone being hauled off to the slammer. The guy was probably fresh out of jail himself, Lars thought. He calmly but quickly backed out of the space and drove off. He looked into his rearview mirror and noticed that the valet was looking down at his cellphone, typing something into it.

He drove up to the top and handed the parking attendant a $20 bill and his parking ticket stub. The attendant took it, although she seemed more interested in watching a little television in the booth.

Lars pulled out of the lot quickly. He kept checking for any police activity, but he knew they wouldn't arrive for at least a few more minutes if at all. In another few blocks his car entered the freeway north, toward Pasadena. Lars repeatedly looked in his rearview mirror for the first couple miles after leaving the bank. Traffic was eerily light on the normally congested freeways.

"Where are we going?" Pierce asked. "You really are out of your mind if you think I am going to be able to do anything for you."

Lars looked at him in the rearview mirror. What a pompous prick. He chuckled loudly enough for Pierce to hear him. *Let the silence make him even more fearful. That way he'll be more likely to cooperate with me when we get where we are going.*

"Are you going to talk with me at all?" the CEO asked a few seconds later.

This time Lars ignored him completely. He turned on the radio. He was going to mess with this bobble-head until he confessed every single last thing.

CHAPTER 14

"YOU HAVE A choice," Lars said when they were five minutes away from his destination. "Your activities have gotten the attention of a client of mine. That client has deep pockets, and he has directed me to learn as much as I can about who you are involved with and why."

"I really don't know what you are talking about," retorted the executive. "If this is about money—if you want money—just tell me how much you want. Leave my family out of this. I can get you the money you want quickly, how ever much it is that you think I am worth to you."

"If you are thinking this is some sort of kidnap scheme, you are wrong. Dead wrong," Lars calmly replied. "I don't need money. There is no amount of money you can arrange that would cause me to let you go before I get the information that I want."

"I don't have the information you think I have. I would like to help you, but I just don't have the information you need."

"We will see about that," Lars said.

The car carrying the head of CityFargo drove on 210 through Pasadena and turned onto a tree-lined street. It slowed down in front of a yellow house with blue trim. The house was located at the base of the San Gabriel Mountains, immediately north of Los Angeles. The garage door began to open as Lars turned into the driveway. Once Lars drove into the garage, the door closed. He led the CEO through a door in the garage down into the basement. In one corner was a backup power generator and in another was a flat screen TV and camera, a videoconferencing system that could provide high-quality audio/video linkage with anywhere in the world.

Lars sat the CEO down in a large brown recliner chair facing the television. "I couldn't pay for my smoothie last night because of a computer glitch. According to the news, there are widespread computer problems affecting how people can pay for things. I know you are involved, and I want to know everything."

"I am not going to be able to tell you absolutely anything because you have the wrong guy. Are you out of your mind? Let me go now before you do anything that you regret."

Lars flared with anger. This pampered schmuck thought he was a tough guy? He lashed out with a backhanded slap that whipped Pierce's head to one side. "I have details of money transfers between your bank and Srepska. I have emails between you and known Srepska operatives. You aren't going anywhere, so how about you cut the shit and tell me what you are involved with."

The CEO didn't say anything, still reeling from the blow.

From a nearby shelf Lars pulled a favorite pistol of his, a Heckler and Koch VP9.

"You are making a big mistake," Pierce said, eyes widening to a comical degree.

"No, you are making the mistake. I am an expert at what I do. No one knows we are here. The license plate of the car I took down to get you is fake. It will never be traced here. And, the scrambler in my pocket disrupted the video cameras in your office building, so there are no pictures of me coming or leaving your office. And I am in disguise, so the people I talked to will draw a composite picture of someone that looks completely different than I really am." Lars casually raised the gun and sighted it on Pierce's forehead. "Normally, you would have been dead long before now, so count yourself lucky. I just want some information. You don't really want this to take longer and be harder for you than it needs to be."

There was an audible click as he deactivated the safety on the gun. Lars then proceeded to aim it at the CEO's left knee. "Otherwise, you may never walk again."

Beads of sweat dotted the banker's forehead. "Okay, okay. I will tell you what you want to know," the CEO said. "We have a relationship, a purely business relationship, with Srepska. We don't give a hill of beans about whatever Srepska stands for or wants. We technically are not supposed to do business with them because of federal bank regulations that prohibit us from doing business with certain organizations that appear on the list that the U.S. Treasury publishes." He attempted a smile, but Lars only scowled more. "But we find a way to work with—I mean, make money off of—some of these organizations anyway. All of this is run through intermediary accounts in the Caribbean."

"So far so good. What about Srepska in particular?"

"Srepska has fairly free access to our banking network, no different than any other business customer that opens an account with us. Same access as you would have, for that matter. They send and receive money, keep funds safeguarded—you know the whole range of banking services that a company would need. We make a couple million dollars a year off them."

Pierce stopped short, but Lars didn't budge an inch. He continued to stare at the CEO like he was lowlife scum.

"Haven't you heard of the phrase dog eat dog? It's eat or be eaten," the banker pleaded. "If you were the head of a company like I am, and had to answer to your board of directors that constantly wants to hear you tell them that your company is growing profits, you would do things you might later regret too. It's just a fact of life. You wouldn't understand it unless you were in my shoes."

Lars didn't need a lecture about the necessities of business. He, in fact, had attended Loyola Law School in Los Angeles. He was

ranked near the top of his class, and completed a judicial clerkship with a federal judge, also a Loyola alum. He did fine at the
clerkship, and the judge offered to introduce him to some of his
classmates who were hiring partners for big law firms. But Lars
decided that the practice of law was too dry and boring for him.

"What else can we expect from your *friends*?" Lars asked with
a smirk.

"I don't really know. My bank just handles their finances. We
don't get involved with the business of our customers who don't
have loans with us. We get basic information from them to satisfy
our regulatory requirements that we document certain information
about the customers we do business with. And of course, we use
all information we get to assess ways that we can market and cross-
sale to our customers, but we don't get into their business and try
to know or find out how they earn or spend their money." The
banker tried to spread his hands, then realized they were shackled.
"Think of us like a highway: a highway doesn't ask why someone
is driving on it. We are simply a means to an end for companies to
do business. No different for Srepska as anyone else."

In reply, Lars stepped over to the other side of the basement.
He took various tools off a chain that was hanging above a work-
bench. He then reached up to take the chain down.

"What is that for?" Pierce asked as he started shaking, thinking
Lars was about to swing it at him. "I promise you, I know nothing.
You don't really want to do that."

Lars again chuckled to himself.

He then looped the chain around the CEO's waist and recliner
chair to keep him secure. He looked in a plastic bin and found a
combination lock. He tried several combinations until it opened.
At that point, he locked the chain around the CEO's waist. He
wouldn't be going anywhere without the recliner chair following
him along.

Lars walked upstairs and went to his study. He took out a

bulky satellite phone and dialed a number. Soon, the same deep German voice in Munich that had called him a day earlier picked up the phone.

"You have what?" the voice said.

Lars recounted what had happened over the previous few hours.

"Take what you have found so far and trace it a step further and see where it leads you. If you can find out the mastermind behind Srepska, we will double the amount of money we are going to pay you for your current assignment. But you need to be careful."

"Yeah, right. I was going to go to the authorities and explain that I just kidnapped a high-ranking banking executive and extracted a confession to cybercrimes," Lars said with a sarcastic laugh.

"Remember, we are dealing with a technologically savvy, powerful criminal cabal. We don't know you, you don't know us. If Srepska gets wind of any government trying to put them out of business, they could make life very complicated very fast. I think you can understand why Germany doesn't want any breadcrumbs leading from you to us. So, you go work on your own. Don't contact us until you are done."

This would be an easy task for Lars. He had applied for a criminal investigator job at the U.S. Department of Homeland Security shortly after law school. He was hired, and soon found himself completing several weeks of law enforcement training. He found himself working in investigations of money-laundering cases. His first cases as a special agent involved tracing money relating to international trade fraud and smuggling. He worked at the job for five years. The fact that he had received several awards and coached newer employees was a badge of honor for him at the time.

But he then became entangled in a murder when he was on a short-term overseas assignment for his job. He had to shoot an officer in Costa Rica's law enforcement agency who was assigned to work with him on a case. Lars had discovered the agent was on the payroll of the trafficker they were investigating. Plus, the agent was an arrogant prick who greatly annoyed Lars by his condescending and arrogant attitude.

His boss, in the interest of preserving relationships between the U.S. and Costa Rica, directed Lars to continue collaborating with the corrupt agent and not to let on that he knew he was compromised. Lars was told that he would be pulled off the mission as soon as it was practical to do so, and the federal government would find another strategy to stop the trafficker. But Lars was angry. Several days later, he shot and killed his colleague as he was on his way home. No one ever fingered Lars, although his boss had a suspicion that he was responsible. But unknown to Lars, the agent he shot was being tailed by a rival crime syndicate who saw that Lars was responsible. A couple weeks later, after Lars had returned to his regular duty station, he was approached on his run by a stranger who knew what Lars had done and offered him a sizable sum of money for a similar job.

Lars denied any knowledge about what the man was talking about and turned down the offer. Yet he worked for his agency for only 10 months after that, until he decided he could make more money by operating his own business as an investigator using the skills he learned through his job at Homeland Security, combined with his law degree.

There were also cruder methods of persuasion. Lars retrieved a laptop from a couch nearby and placed it in Pierce's lap. "Tell you what. You are going to show me exactly what transactions you've had with Srepska. By the time we get through here, I want to know everything you know about them."

CHAPTER 15

LATE THAT AFTERNOON, across the country, the phone rang in a conference room in the nation's central bank. While most people thought of the Fed as controlling inflation, it also had lesser-known responsibilities, such as overseeing the nation's payments system. The room had several large flat-screen TVs monitoring financial and television channels, a Bloomberg terminal, and several cubicles. It also included clocks that reflected the time in major cities across the globe. In the center of the clocks stood one that had the placard "Washington, DC" above it.

On the other end of the phone were executives from MasterCard.

"We are having massive problems with our network. No transactions can be sent or received. As you know, that means no purchases can be made using our cards. We don't know why. The problem was initially localized to one part of California, in a community near Los Angeles. But now the problem that we thought was isolated seems to have expanded more broadly across the United States."

Other calls were coming in constantly, all with the same message: unless it was the old-fashioned paper variety, there was no guarantee that money could be transacted.

Dale Williams, the manager in charge of monitoring the markets, went to conduct an impromptu briefing of the Federal

Reserve Board governor who was responsible for overseeing supervision of the financial system, Betsy Platt. He walked into her office, but there was no one sitting at the secretary's desk. The clock on the wall showed 7:00 p.m. Yet Williams heard a TV in the spacious office where the executive was working. He noticed several boxes stacked inside. Williams spoke softly at the door and Platt quickly told him to come in.

"As you know, market participants know that they are supposed to self-report problems to their regulator no matter how obvious the problems are. We have received phone calls from several of the major payment networks indicating widespread systemic problems impacting the stability of the payment platforms."

"You mean no one can swipe their debit or credit card," Platt said in an attempt to put into common English what the bureaucratic staffer was saying. She began thinking about how the Federal Reserve had responsibility for providing oversight to ensure that the problem was resolved quickly. She knew that it would only be a matter of time before the media and Congressional officials would start to question the quality of the Federal Reserve's supervisory oversight. After all, Platt knew while they weren't banks, the Federal Reserve had authority over VISA and MasterCard since they provide key services to banks, not the least of which is issuing debit and credit cards on their networks.

"Yes. We are scrambling to get to the bottom of the problem. As you know, these firms are required to have contingency plans for how they will maintain continuity of operations in circumstances such as these."

"How exactly will they will keep the lights on when the power goes out?" Governor Platt said in an increasingly frustrated tone, trying to cut through the long-winded staffer's analysis and get to the bottom of what, if any, the Federal Reserve's response would be.

"Well, all that contingency planning really paid off, didn't it?"

she said with a sarcastic laugh. "What are we going to do about it now?"

"We will dispatch examiners to join staff from other regulatory agencies and law enforcement officials at the operations centers of the payment processers and other key financial firms. We will consult with the FBI's infrastructure protection working group and conduct an impact assessment on the economy. We will get started right away, provided you concur."

"Right away is not soon enough," she said. "I need this problem resolved by yesterday."

The staffer remained standing there. Sheepishly he said, "And there is more. As you are very well aware from your recent confirmation hearing briefings, the Federal Reserve System operates the bigger of the two processors of automated clearinghouse (ACH) transactions. Our Atlanta office that manages our ACH processing service just had all their computer servers go offline. They are trying to reboot them now, but they keep getting error messages. Until then, as you can imagine, many other types of monetary transfers won't be able to take place until this gets resolved."

The television in Platt's office was tuned to a financial news channel, which showed breaking coverage of the problem. News updates scrolling across the screen showed that several politicians had used social media to capitalize on the moment to tweet a call for tighter regulation of the nation's financial system, while talk radio hosts found another reason to advocate for a more laissez-faire approach to government control of private enterprise.

"Politicos certainly don't lose an opportunity to make hay," Platt commented to her staffer. She continued to think of the fact that three out of four everyday purchases at merchants or other stores were made with debit or credit cards. A recent briefing had reported how many people do not carry much cash, which made the fact that ATMs are out of service worse. And she feared much larger problems to the economy from the ACH system problems, since trillions of dollars of money moved through it every day. It could not go down for long before people started losing confidence in the banking system, since it was the network through which banks facilitate their customers making payroll and the vast majority of checks get processed. She thought of how these days, most checks are converted to electronic checks and go through the ACH system.

She turned to her deputy. "Perhaps the savings advocates of the world can now have a grand party. There won't be any unnecessary weekend spending," she remarked with her dry sense of humor. "Tell you what. Have someone research the full range of options given to us by the laws passed after the last financial crisis."

Platt began thinking of how the Dodd-Frank Act gave the Federal Reserve and other regulators additional powers over certain financial companies that were essentially utilities for the financial system. They provided basic services so important to the financial system that any disruptions could threaten the economy.

In the interim, they approved a short press release for release at 5:00 p.m.:

The Federal Reserve Board is aware that the processors of credit and debit card transactions are reporting a temporary cessation of operations because of technical problems. Until these problems are resolved, merchants will not be able to electronically facilitate credit and debit card transactions. Merchants should not be alarmed, nor do they need to contact their bank, as these problems are being dealt with systemically.

Additionally, the Federal Reserve System and the other major automated clearinghouse (ACH) operator are temporarily unable to process other types of electronic money transactions, including direct deposits of payroll, most ATM transactions, and electronic clearing of checks.

In the interim, market participants are encouraged to use cash for transactions since debit cards, credit cards, ATM cards, checks, and money transfers may not be possible. The Federal Reserve will ensure sufficient liquidity by dispatching additional cash to Federal Reserve Banks, which will in turn ensure that all banks in their districts have adequate supplies of cash.

However, the Federal Reserve and U.S. Department of Treasury are also investigating reports that some financial institutions are experiencing computer problems that may temporarily impact the ability of depositors to make transactions, including deposits and withdrawals. Depositors are reminded that deposit accounts continue to be insured by the federal government—Federal Deposit Insurance Corporation for banks and National Credit Union Administration for credit unions—and the federal government will ensure that all depositors have access to their money as soon as is practically possible.

The Federal Reserve Board is monitoring the situation and will act as needed to mitigate any adverse effects on the economy from the disruptions.

"One more thing," Platt said. "Remember all the work the financial industry did to prepare for Y2K years ago? We needed to be ready to continue business as usual even if computers malfunction. It should only be a matter of twelve to twenty-four hours before we can get everything back to normal."

CHAPTER 16

FREDRIC HAD BIKED as far west as Vienna, Virginia, when he saw a café at the end of a small strip mall that was open. He was hungry after thirty miles of riding, and he couldn't resist stopping in an American town named Vienna. He stopped and leaned his bike up out front and opened the door to enter. Walking in, he saw people gathered around a TV with news coverage about the problems with the nation's payment system.

He ordered a tea and bagel and paid cash. He sat and watched news as he was pondering his next move.

The Under Secretary for Domestic Finance at the Treasury Department, Audrey Dial, was convening a press conference. The banner scrolling on the TV screen noted, "Watch the press conference of the acting head of the Treasury Department." A white-haired female figure wearing a dark suit walked up to the podium. She opened the notebook that she had been carrying and took a sip of water from the podium before beginning to speak.

"Good afternoon. I am honored to be here. As you know, the U.S. Senate earlier today confirmed Neal Wolman as the next Secretary of the Treasury, and his swearing-in ceremony, scheduled tomorrow, is going to be moved up and take place this evening.

"We are aware that there are unfolding developments that could have serious implications on the financial system. We are working with our colleagues in law enforcement to find the cause.

"The Treasury's Office of Terrorist Financing and Financial Crimes is currently in the process of identifying the threat. Let me be clear: what is happening is the work of a criminal or criminals. It is far too early to speculate whether these disruptions in the marketplace are the work of terrorists. We simply don't have enough information to suggest whether it is or not. But one thing is clear: we will hold those responsible accountable for their actions.

"This is an unprecedented problem. In my twenty-four years serving this nation, I have seen us be tested with the unexpected, and each time we pass the test with flying colors. It will be no different this time around."

She then closed her notebook and walked away from the podium and out the side door from which she came without taking any questions.

Fredric strolled outside afterward, thinking over what the news report had said. It didn't add much to what he already knew. Frustrated that he could not act on his suspicions, he called Schneider, his boss, and explained that he wasn't leaving the U.S.

"Fredric, remember I told you to come back as soon as you made the hand-off."

"I was planning to do exactly that, but when I left Lim's office, this woman came in immediately after and started talking about some deal they had made. I couldn't find out what she meant because at that moment Lim's busybody secretary shut the door in my face." Fredric was growing angrier as he talked. "Look, I already have a base of knowledge about how Srepska works. I might be able to help the American authorities."

Schneider gave a huge sigh, and Fredric knew what that meant. "I agree that the timing does look peculiar. All right, you stay on the scene, find out what you can. But you know the drill—don't do anything that might put you, and us, in jeopardy for foreign surveillance activities on U.S. soil. Stay low. Don't call me again until you are back home."

"Understood."

Just then his phone rang. *I sure hope I bought enough minutes for whatever calls I need to have on this phone. I should have bought more minutes after I landed.*

"This is Attorney General Jason Lim."

Fredric was startled by his calling so soon after Fredric had been discussing him. "Yes, can I be of help to you?"

"Fredric, I need to tell you something that is very important. But you have to promise that you will not say a word to anyone about this conversation. Deal?"

"Deal." *Of course. But what does he mean?*

"It's really best if we do this in person. Can you meet?"

"Why? Everything I had, I left with you. I don't have anything else."

"No, it's not about what you brought. Well, actually, it is. It's hard to explain over the phone." Lim stopped short, and Fredric glanced all around him, making sure no one was listening in. "Okay," Lim went on, "I know this is difficult to believe, but you have to trust me. I will get right to the point and not beat around the bush. There is something really weird going on. I had to hand over what you gave me to someone who was working for a guy who loaned me money years ago. Years ago. I don't understand why someone in my office suddenly tried to collect the money I owe him. Not just that, but why did this happen out of the blue when I understood repaying the debt was deferred? I just don't understand what happened."

Is this guy serious? Fredric quickly replied, "I gave you confidential information that your people should be able to use to stop this financial manipulation. From what I saw on TV a short while ago, it sure didn't seem like what I handed over was being put to use. Are you saying that it is because you let the information I worked so hard to collect and deliver simply fly out the window?"

"I didn't have any choice in what I did. Well, maybe I did, but then I would be dead and they could get away with whatever they wanted. Let me be perfectly clear: everything you gave me is gone. I—" Lim said before Fredric cut him off.

"Are you completely inept or completely corrupt?" he asked irately. Being proved right about his suspicions didn't help much. They still had to stop these people.

"Yes, I know. I didn't keep my end of the bargain. But give me a second chance. I really can help you. But you have got to trust me and not communicate with anyone else what I am about to tell you. I am calling you from a disposable prepaid phone that cannot be traced to me and that no one knows about. Sensitivity is important."

"Okay, keep talking." *I need to stay professional,* Fredric thought, trying to rein in his temper.

"I don't know where the person who works for me took the information. But I cannot let what I did stand. What exactly did you bring me?" Lim asked.

"I had recorded money transfers and roundabout investments that they are making. They were working long hours. I believe they are very far along, if not almost at end of what they are planning," Fredric replied. "Who took the information? Tell me about a loan you took out. Maybe that will help me track them down."

"Nearly thirty years ago, after I finished law school at Indiana University, I decided not to go practice law right away, and instead earned a graduate degree in bioengineering at Purdue University. It was a good decision because I made an amazing scientific discovery while a student at Purdue. Shortly after I graduated, I founded a pharmacological firm, Qesys, which focused on conducting research to develop new treatments for heart disease. My firm was able to use my discovery to quickly get a key patent for a drug that became well-used domestically. After building my business and getting rich, I ran for governor of Indiana, a job that I held for eight years."

Fredric started tapping his feet, wondering where this all was going.

"Just after I launched my first campaign for governor, my firm ran into rough times as doctors across the country began to suspect that one of our drugs had serious side effects. We recalled it and stopped selling the product until more research could be conducted. We had other drugs in the pipeline ready to market, but quickly ran short on cash. We didn't want to go public and sell stock. My team wondered if we would have enough money to pay the bills."

"Let me guess, you made a deal with an investor you now regret," Fredric asked.

"Not quite. I was still involved in running my business even while I was running for governor. I didn't sell it until a year after being elected. So, a wealthy Hungarian was introduced to me as a potential source of cash. He was well known in Indianapolis as a wealthy real estate investor. Well-connected, no one knew much about him other than that he was wealthy and still had ties to friends and family in Hungary. But Indianapolis was his adopted city, and he made a big deal about flashing his cash around on social and civic causes. He had given another businessman I knew a loan, and while it was costly, he was discreet. The Hungarian guy gave me a twenty-million-dollar line of credit to keep the business afloat. Since I didn't borrow the money through a bank or other customary channels, no one was ever aware of the loan and everyone assumed that I had been very smart to successfully navigate the firm through a crisis."

"Shortly after I won re-election as Governor, I began campaigning for Bradley Evans after he started his campaign for President. The guy I owed told me to not worry about repaying the debt because of what good my business does for people's health. After all, he knew that I took a pay cut as governor compared to when I was running my business. I just didn't have the same income, or same cash flow, that I had before entering politics. I figured he saw me as his connection to the possible next president and wanted to use that relationship to benefit his business ventures. I figured it was all about access to the possible president's inner circle. Maybe I would invite him as my guest to dinner at the White House, let him get his picture taken with the President, maybe get a little face time with the President to blabber about his favorite cause, you get the picture. In politics, after all, money and access is all the name of the game."

"In your country, I hear it is," Fredric retorted. *This guy is talking fast and sounds really nervous.*

"Fast forward a couple years. Evans gets elected President and appoints me as Attorney General of the United States. The other day I sent an email to my immediate staff saying that an under-cover German operative was coming to deliver information on Srepska. Shortly after, that is when it all happened. The law clerk intern who worked on my team came to remind me of my debt to the Hungarian and tell me that the interest that compounded on the debt meant I owed more than twice the amount than what I originally borrowed. I was shocked. How did she know, and why would she be telling me? I haven't even talked to the guy who loaned me money in a couple years."

Lim sounded distressed, but Fredric was fuming. He could see exactly where this story was going.

"She said that they wanted all their money back. I just don't have that much money to repay the debt. I could sell some investments, but it would raise questions in the media. And quite frankly, this is a lot of money even to me."

Fredric didn't think the timing was any accident. "The Hungarian who loaned you money was part of Srepska. The leaders of Srepska didn't want or need your loan to be repaid after you got a Cabinet-level position. They hit the lottery when it was you to whom they loaned money. They had plans to use the money as a blackmail strategy. The chief law enforcement official of the world's largest economy was suddenly their tool," Fredric said with a sarcastic laugh. *These people are good,* Fredric thought.

Lim spoke. "I know, Fredric, you may not trust me. But you have to. I am laying open my soul to help stop these people. I haven't been on the job for very long as Attorney General, and I don't want this to be how people remember me. If I go to the FBI, what I just told you is going to get out sooner or later and my career will be over. I hope you understand why I am turning to you to help me."

Fredric wasn't interested in his sob story. He had a more pressing matter at hand. "How can I find the intern who took the materials?"

"I have a copy of her resume from our human resources office. Her resume lists an address in Philadelphia. Here it is…"

Fredric repeated back the address. 2435 South Street. *I can remember that.*

"How far away is Philadelphia from Washington…it's only a couple hours away, right?"

Lim chuckled. "Maybe in Germany where you have those interstates with no speed limits, you would be able to go the distance between here and Philadelphia that fast. It is almost three hours, and that's not counting traffic."

Fredric was calculating the closest place to rent a car when Lim continued. "Listen, I can get you plugged into the people who are trying to sort things out. You probably don't have a lot of faith in the U.S. Department of Justice after what just happened, and I don't really know who I can trust on my team. I am new here. Maybe you can hook up with your buddies in the CIA or NSA or even the military. Maybe you can talk to the investigators at the FBI or Treasury Department or Federal Reserve Board who are sorting out the mess with the payment system. I'll help you get wherever you need to be."

Fredric thought about the offer. True, these people can get me access to information quickly. *But how could I trust that they are competent and dedicated to the mission. I would prefer working alone to working with some unknowns in America that some guy who doesn't seem very trustworthy wants to connect me to.* After a long silence, he told Lim lightheartedly, "I think I am going to trust my instincts and let your guys do their thing and I will do mine."

CHAPTER 17

WITH THE MUTED clacking of computer keys the large room might have been the office of a start-up company. The seven men and one woman were all dressed casually, down to the half-filled coffee cups that littered the desk and conference table. Yet their faces looked far from placid, or drawn with the usual sagging that nine-to-five days bring. Oddly, everyone was sweating. That was not because the thermostat was turned up too high. It was even a little chilly, due to a cheap boss. No, what produced the beads of sweat on everybody's forehead was the pressure they were under. The pressure of bringing the entire United States economy to its knees.

Pacing the room was a man whose white hair set him distinctly apart from the fresh faces of his employees. His eyes probed every screen, making sure the audacious scam was proceeding as he had designed it. He knew it was foolproof. Hadn't they already brought the miserable country of Kenya to its knees? As he had told his subordinates before, more times than they wanted to hear, "The principles are the same. We are just scaling up." He chuckled as he thought of that now. Just scaling up. To the big time. To the biggest of all time.

His good humor was broken by the ring tone of his cellphone. He'd had it programmed to "Dot Your Eyes." As the singer belted out, "...and cross your fucking teeth," he clicked on the caller.

"Natasha? Do you have the data?"

"Yes, I will be sending it momentarily, Zoltan. I had to go crosstown to our secure site, and the traffic in this city is terrible."

Zoltan had no interest in her troubles. "Send it immediately. We must find out what that German spy discovered. He has already caused us enough trouble."

Her voice became concerned. "I just reviewed it, and he stole some valuable data of ours. I don't know what sort of technical ability he has, but if he sent it to the BND, they certainly have people there who could track us down."

Zoltan felt a sudden surge in his heartbeat. His chest felt too full, as though he would burst. Yet once he fully took in her news, he found a new calm. "They cannot untangle the cryptology that quickly, if they can penetrate it at all. By the time they could, our work in America will already be finished."

"If you say so." She was clearly worried, perhaps by her exposure in the country.

"Why don't you send it to me," he said, his voice growling with increasing impatience, "so I can see what the hell you have?"

"Yes, of course. I am sending it right now."

As he waited for the transmission, he thought through the next steps in the plan. In another hour, the planned abduction of the U.S. president would be carried off. That part seemed solid. The substitution of his doppelganger was more problematic. Looks alone would not be enough. Yet their plant only had to fool the Americans long enough for their plans to go through. If he was then captured, even killed, that wasn't Zoltan's problem.

Natasha's voice came back on the line. "Okay, I've sent them all."

"That's very good. I'll take a look at it right away. But don't you fret, our plans are moving forward, and no one can stop us. Do you understand?"

"Y-yes, I-I do."

"No one!" he thundered. "We cannot be stopped. Do you understand?"

This time her reply was more emphatic. "Yes, perfectly. So, I should proceed to the next step?"

"Yes, get up to Philadelphia and join the others. The next phase in ruining the United States is about to begin."

CHAPTER 18

PRESIDENT BRADLEY EVANS was in the Oval Office, watching the unfolding developments as he was briefed on the situation by Peter Campbell, his Chief of Staff. "What should I be doing?" he asked.

"It is not clear that there *is* anything you can do," was the reply. "We are in contact with the FBI to stay abreast of their progress. They assure me they are devoting every resource at their disposal to resolve the situation. I am pressing them to give me status updates throughout the day. Just so you know, Mr. President, they warned this may still take several days to unravel." He checked his phone to see what time it was. "And Neal Wolman is scheduled to be sworn in as Treasury Secretary in about thirty minutes. As you requested, you are on the program for his swearing-in ceremony. Shall I tell his office that you will not be able to make it?"

"No, definitely not. Neal was my roommate during my freshman year in college, and we have so much history together. He's been there for me so many times over the years, you bet that I will be the one to administer the oath of office to him. I want to have a small ceremony—I don't want a full entourage to go with me."

"Yes, sir, I understand. We should be leaving soon. The press will be in the room, and based on the media advisory from a couple days ago, the media will be expecting you to be there. I warn you, they will probably use the opportunity to ask you about what is happening. I wouldn't answer any questions about the current situation until we know more. We don't know if it is a terrorist attack or a rogue hacker somewhere. If we guess wrong or your words get misinterpreted, we will have an even bigger mess on our hands, because investors both here and overseas will get spooked. Remind them that we will be scheduling a separate press briefing to address this situation and don't say more."

"So we should leave now," the President asked.

"Yes. It is a short walk over. Nice weather outside," Chief of Staff Campbell said. "The President is ready to go to the Treasury Department," he announced to the two Secret Service agents who were standing in the doorway.

"It is my first full week on the job and things are completely not like I expected them to go after inauguration," the President muttered as he was getting up.

The President soon was walking out of the White House and through a secured courtyard over to the Treasury Building. He went into a side door of the Treasury Department facing the White House, which was being held open for him by the Secret Service agents.

The walk took merely a minute, all behind the tall perimeter fence that separates the White House and Treasury Department from countless visitors taking pictures. A TV news crew captured the President's trip over through the security gate, even though it was starting to get dusk.

Once the President got inside the Treasury Department, he walked up three flights on a wide, ceremonial spiral staircase.

He entered a large chamber that had been converted into a war room. Several large flat-screen televisions sat on rolling carts for the Treasury officials to monitor the news. The large table was dwarfed by the empty space around it. More than a dozen people in suits were standing around looking at the computers and talking. A few others seemed to be glued to watching the unfolding developments on the televisions. Some of the men had loosened ties and were staring at their BlackBerry phones. At least three men were wearing freshly pressed uniforms with badges on their chests and guns on their waists.

Once the President walked in, the men sitting around the table with the soon-to-be Treasury Secretary all stood. The President shook some hands and quickly walked with Neal Wolman and Under Secretary for Domestic Finance Dial to a small room next door to discuss the problem.

"Mr. President, we are actively investigating the problem," Dial said. "No one knows yet much about the unfolding developments."

"I bet you that extreme environmental activists engineered this attack as a political statement about what they consider to be the rapid growth of capitalism and its impact on global warming," Wolman said.

"No. I'll bet it is some terrorist organization from the Middle East," Dial responded.

"Well, these theories are based exclusively on still-developing internet chatter, so it is too early to draw any conclusions. Law enforcement is in the very early stages of this investigation, and we will know more soon," the President counseled.

A young man who barely looked twenty-one, wearing a white shirt and red tie, knocked on the door. "Everything is ready for the ceremony when you are," the eager face cheerfully said.

The President joined the soon-to-be Treasury Secretary as they walked down the hall to a large ceremonial room that had six large television cameras stationed at the back. A row with a sign that read "press" was filled with a half dozen reporters. At the front was a podium flanked on either side by large comfortable chairs.

As expected, the President administered the oath of office to Wolman. "I am so proud of you serving our country in this new role," he said. "There will be ups and downs, for sure, but nothing that you won't be able to handle." When he finished speaking, everyone politely applauded his kind remarks.

Just then fire alarms went off in the building. The shrieking was so loud, it made talking difficult. A recorded message warned, "An emergency has been reported. Please proceed to the nearest stairwell and exit the building. Do not use the elevators." Flashing strobe lights on the alarms were even more distracting than the sirens.

Following established protocol, Secret Service agents confirmed both whether the alarm was legitimate and the proper route to leave the building. All indications were that it was a false alarm. Perhaps the only issue was overcooked popcorn in a microwave that activated the sensitive fire-prevention system in the building. They discussed whether to err on the side of caution and take the President back to the White House. Particularly since the President had accomplished the purpose of his trip over to the Treasury Building.

Within a minute, sirens could be heard in the background. Two fire trucks and a large box-shaped hazardous materials fire truck pulled around a corner. They parked in front of a door that said, "Fire control room." The first firefighter off the trucks tugged on the door lined with metal bars, but it was locked.

He walked back to the truck while a group of eight other firefighters walked up the street and in the front door of the Treasury Department Building. They were all carrying big long bags with the words "DC Fire" stenciled on the side, presumably filled with hoses and other firefighting equipment. The bags looked eerily similar to body bags, yet they had briefcase-like carrying straps on the side.

Meanwhile, one firefighter stood outside and proceeded to take a hose off the fire truck and attached it to a sprinkler connection on the side of the building.

As soon as the team of firefighters entered the Treasury Building, one firefighter went to check the monitor and a control monitor for the building's fire prevention system, located a few feet from the front door. Whether coincidentally or not, suddenly the sprinklers started to activate in the Treasury Department on all floors. A fine mist increased to a steady pour of water.

"It is in zone five," the firefighter looking at the panel shouted to his colleagues. "Can you unlock the door to the fire control room?" another firefighter shouted to a Secret Service guard who was standing watching. He used his walkie-talkie to pass the request on to another agent.

The group of firefighters hurried to the other end, completely opposite the side of the building where their truck was parked. They stopped near the set of doors that lead out to the White House through a secured, access-restricted courtyard. Two Secret Service agents were guarding the door, sitting at a security booth. Two firefighters rapidly approached the two guards.

"Hey, where is the sprinkler control room in this building?" they asked.

Suddenly one agent fell to the floor. Soon, the other agent was also lying down. The firefighters were holding a small stun gun that made hardly a sound. Two firefighters then quickly approached the agents and injected them with a strong dose of ketamine, a powerful sedative that would cause the agents to remain unconscious for several hours. Then they quickly dragged their bodies behind the little security booth near the doors so they would not be immediately visible.

They didn't need to worry about the surveillance cameras capturing what was happening because the sprinklers had gotten the cameras wet and rendered them useless. From the security control room where presumably one or more guards were watching the dozens of cameras monitoring the Treasury Building's hallways and outer perimeter, the monitors would just be showing blobs of movement, without enough detail for those watching the monitors to tell exactly what was happening.

The firefighters then moved to a vent in front of the stairwell. They stood there as if something was wrong with it. "There is smoke up there," the firefighter on his knees shouted to his colleagues.

Within a minute, they heard people running down the steps.

Upstairs, the Secret Service agents decided to move the President back to the White House quickly given that the water from the sprinklers was starting to accumulate on the floor.

The President and the Secret Service agents accompanying him walked briskly down the circular staircase from the upper floors. The staircase stopped directly in front of the side door facing the White House.

As the President and his three Secret Service bodyguards were coming down the stairs, the team of firefighters was ready to greet them. Not with smiles, but with stun guns. Immediately the four Secret Service agents and the President dropped to the floor, losing consciousness. Again, the firefighters had their syringes ready. With a quick injection, they effectively incapacitated the President and his bodyguards.

Meanwhile, one of the firefighters who was standing behind the others shrugged off his firefighter's uniform. Suddenly he was wearing a dark suit, freshly pressed light blue shirt, and blue tie. He looked nearly identical to President Evans, with hair the same color and length, thanks to a combination of plastic surgery and cosmetic enhancements. He took the pin off the President's jacket and put it on his own. He checked the President's pockets and only found a wallet. The double took it and put it in his own pocket.

Meanwhile, three other firefighters were also taking off their firefighter uniforms and stuffing these coveralls into duffel bags. They revealed dark suits and white shirts beneath their uniforms. These firefighters then converged on the three Secret Service agents who had been guarding the President and took their radios, keys, phones, jacket pins, and other equipment. They took off the earpieces and put them in their own ears. They took off the radios from the Secret Service agents and threaded the microphones from the agents through their jacket sleeves so they would rest on the wrist with a piece of tape. The other five firefighters bound the sleeping Secret Service agents' hands and legs and placed them into the large bags.

The five firefighters still wearing their uniforms then proceeded to walk around to the other side of the floor. They found the fire control room. There were two Secret Service agents standing by it.

"Is there a fire?" one asked the first firefighter.

"Should we get everyone evacuated ASAP?" the Agent responded.

The firefighters then went into the fire control room. They dropped their bags and opened the door that led to the street where their fire trucks were parked. One by one they lowered the bags outside the door. Opening the door had caused a high-pitched alarm to sound, but it was more than drowned out by the louder sound of the fire alarms throughout the building. Two firefighters then carried the people into the truck. The other three firefighters went back inside and found the door that they came in. One firefighter then went to the control box, and suddenly the sprinklers and alarms stopped.

"Good news, this is a false alarm. There is no fire, no gas leak, no carbon monoxide problems," one of the firefighters told the Secret Service agents near the front door. "Looks like there was just a massive malfunction of the equipment. Tell your building engineers that they had better do an overhaul and fix whatever caused this problem, probably a faulty heat sensor on the first floor in the east sector of the building from what we saw on the building's fire monitoring system and then we confirmed it by looking in the vent. And let them know that this false alarm brought three engines down here and risked the safety of pedestrians as we sped here, not to mention that we took our time checking out a false alarm when there could have been other emergencies happening at the same time."

One of the firefighters' radio then beeped and a muffled voice began to mumble. "Hey we have another call to get to, a fire in a condo near DuPont Circle," a firefighter shouted to the two firefighters who were talking to the Secret Service agents. "It is time to go. You all get your building engineers to get the problem fixed and have someone clean up the water."

"All the other guys left the building already through another door and are on the truck. We have got to go," a firefighter volunteered to the Secret Service agents.

The Secret Service agents thanked them, and the firefighters walked out the doors and back to their trucks. With sirens blaring, the three trucks proceeded to race down the street to their next call.

Meanwhile, on the opposite side of the building from where the fire truck was speeding away, the former firefighter now playing the role of President Evans was walking through the doors to exit the Treasury Building with the former firefighters, now dressed and acting as Secret Service agents, following. The new President Evans then walked through the courtyard toward the White House.

"That went well," said one of the false agents to his rear.

The fake president was not so cheery. "That was the easy part. Now I have to run the country."

CHAPTER 19

THEY APPROACHED THE White House. The real Secret Service agents standing at the doors of the guardhouse in the secured area between the Treasury Department and White House quickly opened the gate. The group continued to briskly walk forward. Other Secret Service agents soon opened the doors for the group to enter the White House. All the way to the East Wing, agents repeatedly opened doors for them to pass through.

As the President was walking into the Oval Office, he stopped at the desk of his assistant in a little room just outside. *This looks so much smaller than what I was expecting from the pictures,* he thought. The President ordered a convening of a video conference with the national security team within forty-five minutes.

"I want to participate in the meeting via video from the underground command center for security reasons." The President began thinking through what he had rehearsed repeatedly. *So far, so good,* he thought.

"Yes, Mr. President. This will be your first video conference here at the White House. It is similar to what I am sure you experienced on the campaign trail, just higher quality, and the room will probably be larger than what you are used to."

"I need to make an important call to a foreign leader in a couple of minutes. I want to go down to the safe room downstairs right now, and I don't want anyone coming with me other than you and these two Secret Service agents. I just got back from the Treasury Department, and there was a fire in the building. Someone is declaring war on the United States, and until we know more, I need to be in the most secure location possible."

The assistant placed a call. "Okay, I will lead you to the safe room. The people who can let you in are coming."

This doesn't sound good, the imposter President thought. *More people means more risk that I will be detected. I hope that the team got out of the other building and is well on their way back. If they got caught, I will get caught too.*

Nearly an hour later, the President entered the situation room via teleconference from the secured floor downstairs. One of these Secret Service men walked over to the camera near the large video screen aimed toward the conference room table. He looked up on the screen and recognized the Vice President, National Security Advisor, Defense Secretary, Attorney General Lim, Treasury Secretary, and Intelligence Chief. He noticed other people in the background, and assumed that they were their aides and assistants. *Good job,* the President thought of his comrade's work as he saw on the screen that the camera was aimed on the wall well above where he would be seated.

He sat down at the head of the table. Speaking to the assembled Cabinet members, he said, "I have unexpected news. I just got off the phone with the Prime Minister of Myanmar. He told me that their country is launching an electronic war on the U.S." *Say as few words as possible,* he remembered being told, just as he was about to elaborate on what he just said. He scanned the faces around the table on the screen. Everyone in the room had an incredulous look on his or her face. *We knew this was going to happen, so it is a good sign that this is going to work out as we planned,* he thought.

The Secretary of State chuckled and said, "Are you serious? Myanmar is one of the least developed countries in the world.

The idea that they are behind the sophisticated, well-coordinated attacks on our country's financial system is just not realistic. It's too hard for me to believe."

"The video isn't flowing through, Mr. President," someone in the room said. "You might want to have someone adjust the camera, because it seems to be cutting you off entirely. We just have a good view of the top of the wall near the ceiling."

"Are you kidding me? We are dealing with a possible war here, and you are asking me to waste time on such a trivial matter? I didn't recognize your voice. Who were you who just had that very enlightening comment?" He caught himself as he tried to channel his anger as professionally as possible as he had rehearsed, rather than the cruder way he was used to.

There was a short pause. "This is Mark Cinnamon, Mr. President. My apologies, I…"

The President cut him off. "Get your priorities right, Cinnamon, or next time you are fired."

The cabinet room went silent upstairs. Cinnamon, sitting in for the Secretary of the Transportation Department, looked down sheepishly.

The President shouted, "This is no joke. We are being attacked. Today it is by Myanmar, but we know their military is heavily supported by India and China. With swift, decisive action we can show that we are serious and stop this before it gets any worse."

"I too find this news hard to believe. Myanmar is heavily dependent on our goodwill, Mr. President, as they try to open their country to foreign trade," said the National Security Advisor. "It is not in their economic interest to harm the United States. Besides, I imagine that you could fit in this room the number of people in Myanmar who know enough about computers to do anything even remotely like this, and even then, they would have to have outside help." When the President did not respond, he went on, more nervous, "But North Korea is highly unpredictable.

This could be the work of North Korea, working through Myanmar. But that would have to mean the People's Republic of China was on-board with the plan, and probably lending some expertise, and that I just couldn't speculate about without having some more concrete evidence."

The President then said "Good work. That's what we need more of if we are going to get our country back to normalcy. Mr. Attorney General, I understand your men have proof of this too, isn't that right?" *These people are really gullible,* the imposter thought to himself after hearing the National Security Advisor's analysis. *We are going to get rich if these people invent scenarios like this and create major chaos in the world for a few weeks.*

Lim picked up the glass of water in front of him and took a sip. He looked conflicted by what to do. *This may not be good,* the fake president thought as he clenched his jawbone.

Yet Lim shook his head and meekly said, "Yes, sir, you are right."

The President turned to everyone and further berated them for doubting him. "When I get privileged information, I expect that my Cabinet members will proceed on that basis. Do you think I made up Myanmar's involvement during this terrible crisis?"

The uniformed man behind the Defense Secretary tapped him on the shoulder. The Secretary leaned back as the uniformed assistant whispered into his ear. The Defense Secretary then piped up. "My staff has just informed me that it definitely appears that the electronic attacks on the financial system are originating from a governmental computer network in Myanmar. In fact, I am told that our analysis is suggesting that there is a distinct electronic bread trail to the Chinese government through Myanmar. But these are preliminary reports. We still need to confirm that they are accurate."

The President slammed his fist on the table. The loud thump was clearly audible even across the teleconference. Everyone in the situation room suddenly had a look of fear or concern on their face. The President proceeded to order the Defense Secretary, "I want you to immediately begin to attack strategic Myanmar military targets in retribution. That includes their capital Naypyidaw, Yangon, and Mandalay." As he spoke, he was watching his Cabinet for their reactions. "And prepare for war on China too. It will only be a matter of time."

Alarmed, the Secretary of State spoke up and suggested "Can we seek to resolve this problem through the international community before we so quickly resort to war?"

The President had a quick answer. "No. We need to hit them now before they have time to prepare and harden their resistance. We want to catch them off-guard."

Attorney General Lim offered, "Shouldn't you get approval from Congress before you take military action against another country, or at least brief congressional leaders? You will eventually need to get congressional approval anyway, and I can advise you that it is better to have them feel included from the get-go. Under the powers invested in you—"

The President cut Lim off in an authoritarian voice. "I can do whatever the hell I want. I will call Congressional Leaders shortly to brief them. Get ready now and attack within 96 hours. Let's issue a statement to the press," he shouted to his press secretary.

"Do you want to hold a press conference?" he asked.

"No, I want to issue a statement to the press. It's best they don't know where I am, so I don't want to do it via video or teleconference. And no members of the White House press corps are going to be allowed in the bunker for security reasons."

"But, Mr. President, you are so great in front of the news camera, and what people need to see right now is your face telling them that everything is going to be okay." *No, I don't. If I do that, someone is going to analyze my voice or face and realize what is going on. I cannot get anywhere near the media,* he thought as he looked again at the screen to see how well the camera was still trained on the wall above the conference table.

"I told you what to do. I don't want to tell you again, or I will find someone who can do this job without questioning my instincts. People elected me president, not you."

The press secretary looked stunned.

The President's press secretary soon tweeted that the President would issue a statement for 8:00 that evening to address the unfolding developments. Citizens who were watching their financial lives unravel before their eyes were eager for news—any news—that could shed light on the developments.

"That will be all," he said flatly. "Thank you for attending."

"His reaction to me was so unlike the man I got to know on the campaign trail," he mumbled to his deputy. "He must be having a really bad day. So maybe it's a good thing he doesn't want to go in front of the press," he said with a wisecrack.

Is this going to be World War III if China gets involved, the press secretary thought.

He walked into the office of Peter Campbell, the White House Chief of Staff, and asked, "Have you talked with the President? I am really worried about him. He didn't seem his normal self when I spoke to him before he went to the secure underground bunker. And what just happened during our impromptu cabinet meeting is beyond me. I never knew him to be rude or short with people like he was during the meeting. Too bad he didn't want to join us up here above ground in person."

"Funny thing you should ask," Campbell said. "He's the boss, but I am still trying to figure out why he went down there with just two Secret Service agents, not the rest of us who I would have thought he would want to be consulting with face to face."

"How about the Vice President? Has she spoken to the President?" the press secretary asked.

"She spoke to him on the phone, but only briefly. She said he didn't sound his normal self. He is perhaps overwhelmed with all that is happening. We talked about it and we concluded that the President is not a great delegator, so it is reasonable to expect him to issue these ultimatums to the rest of us from his secure location. They always say you see what a man is made of in how he responds to a crisis, and I guess his normal calm nature has temporarily given way to a reclusive, on-edge personality."

"Is he medically okay? The Secret Service guys can probably assess that," the press secretary said.

"Good thought, I will go ask the lead agent on duty. He also got left above ground, by the way. I can try to persuade the President when he calms down to let me and the White House physician down there. And even if he doesn't, if push comes to shove, access to that bunker is controlled by biometric scans, and I am one of the people who can get in—unless they activated the mechanism to irreversibly lock it from inside." They both paused at this disturbing thought. Could the new president be so unhinged by the crisis that he would do that?

Outside the White House, the skies were dark. Americans without cash were unable to purchase gas, buy groceries, or make other everyday purchases at pharmacies or other stores. Even those with cash were unable to make purchases at many stores that had a credit/debit card reader connected to the electronic cash register. For some technical reason beyond the manager's knowledge, many cash registers had locked up and were unusable.

Grocery store lines were long as cashiers struggled to make exact change for those who were paying in cash. Gas stations had longer than usual lines as everyone who wanted to buy gas had to pay cash with the cashier. ATMs had blank screens or simply said "Out of Service." That meant that other than at cash-only businesses, generally small businesses, business could not be conducted.

Most Americans could without doubt survive a few weeks without the ability to use ATM or debit cards. Just a few blocks from the White House, though, one young man kicked the self-checkout machine at a pharmacy where he could not buy the diapers for his child. As he ripped the "Cash Only" sign off of the machine, a store employee rushed over and said, "Calm down, sir."

"This isn't right," he shouted.

Another person dressed in brown construction boots and a heavy work jacket trying to buy a six-pack yelled, "Tell me about it."

Another employee came out from behind the counter. "I am terribly sorry but we can only accept cash."

The first man slammed his elbow into the self-checkout computer terminal. Everyone gasped as the screen cracked. The employees began to back away as the man who came behind the counter reached for the telephone.

"Enough is enough. You all can afford to have a hundred per-cent off day once in a while," another lady said as she walked out the front door pushing a shopping basket.

The man who smashed the screen tossed a rack of bananas in the direction of the cashier. He ducked. The sound of the loud rack clanging on the floor brought more people up front.

"We are closed. Everyone leave the store," a manager wearing a white shirt shouted as he came out from the back.

Someone else threw a big bag of mini-Snickers candy at his feet.

Suddenly, two other people grabbed shopping bags and began filling them.

Several men rushed toward the shelves and started grabbing everything in sight. When the manager came toward them, yell-ing, "You can't do that!" one of the men whirled around. In his hand appeared a handgun.

"Why don't you try stopping me?"

The manager, along with all of the employees, hurried to the back room, locking the door behind them.

CHAPTER 20

"WHO GIVES YOU your orders? How can I reach them?" Lars demanded of bank president Marvin Pierce.

"I don't really know. It's just a business relationship I have with them. I have never met them, just exchanged a couple of phone calls. It wasn't a smart decision, but hey, it's not the first time that someone bent the rules to make a little extra money. Are you telling me you haven't ever done that yourself?"

Lars flared at the implication that he tried to cheat people. "I don't appreciate being accused of things I don't do. You are going to tell me everything you know. I don't have time to be talked to like I am a naive police detective. I am not. I am the person who will decide whether you walk out of here alive. I am not going to ask you again."

"I told you, I don't know anything that can help you."

When Lars heard that, he'd had enough. He retrieved a syringe and filled it with a small amount of sodium amytal. He made a big show of it, and sure enough, the banker was watching with horror. Lars walked over and slowly gave the tied-up CEO an injection as he frantically yelled, "What are you doing?"

Lars put the syringe aside, took the gloves off, and leaned on a table as he glanced up to the large flat-screen TV hanging on his wall in the basement. He saw the CNN logo on the lower bar of the screen, which featured a medium-sized photo of the President. A CNN anchor was reading the president's statement.

"Today Myanmar, also known as Burma, attacked the U.S. They may not have used weapons, but the devastation and disruption felt in communities across the country is the same. The ability of Americans to meet their everyday financial needs has been disrupted because of a war declared on us by a diabolical country half the world away. Myanmar has declared economic war on us. They have declared war on our way of life. And we have reason to believe that they are backed and supported by North Korea and the People's Republic of China. Whether they did this to gain an economic advantage in the world or just because they envy the great success of our country, we do not know. As the leader of this great country, I will not let this stand."

Lars was stunned by the broadcast. President Bradley Evans had announced that America was preparing for war, with air strikes on major cities in Myanmar within the week. Aircraft carriers in the Pacific were being transitioned for a war that would likely soon involve China and North Korea as well. There was no time for the traditional congressional approval of the war before it took place, he explained. U.S. military leadership was needed right away.

The TV program then switched to the Pentagon press room. Several uniformed men entered and took up positions around the podium. Soon an analyst was interviewed. "A small well-trained group of computer hackers from North Korea could be involved with what is happening," one of them said.

Lars wasn't sure what to make of the announcement. Myanmar was a developing country and he had recently read an article reporting that rolling power outages were the norm. Could Srepska be betting against the Myanmar currency? Lars wondered.

The timer went off on his tablet computer. He thought of how quickly five minutes had passed when he was watching TV.

"Who else knows about the money transfers from Srepska? How can I find someone who works for Srepska?"

Under the influence of the drug, the banker was more forthcoming. "I can tell you the address of where the person works. Go to my Blackberry and look up the address for a Keir Dalton. That is the person who contacted me some time back to set up the account, and he is the person who uses the account. He works for an old guy overseas who I never met, but I know he was telling this Dalton guy what to do."

Lars opened up the Blackberry and found the address. Dalton was located at 2435 South Street in Philadelphia. So why had he contacted a banker all the way out in L.A.?

"I can also tell you about the other special needs accounts that we opened. Law enforcement officials wouldn't be too happy about this because of their ties to narcotics trafficking in Latin America and online gambling. Would you be interested in those?"

The truth serum was working. But Lars was focused on the challenge at hand.

He considered how difficult it would be to get from Los Angeles to Philadelphia at a time of financial pandemonium. He could not expect to easily refuel at a gas station if he drove his car, and it would be impossible to purchase an airline ticket because of the payment network problems. Besides, the person at the address was likely a mere flunky and wouldn't be very helpful in the grand scheme of resolving the situation, he realized.

His thoughts shifted to previous military interventions by the United States, and he figured he only had a few days in which to resolve the situation before attacks on Myanmar would take place. *But how?* he wondered.

Reading the *Washington Post* website, he noticed a news blog posting about a malfunction in the Treasury Department's sprinkler system that caused massive water damage in the building. The DC Fire Department said that they didn't have a record of a fire call at the Treasury Department, although the Treasury spokesperson said that everyone remembered fire trucks there. This seemed like small potatoes compared to the bigger problems happening that day, and the DC Fire Department spokesperson admitted that it was possible that the call took place and just didn't get recorded properly, a problem that wouldn't have been unusual, given their record-keeping problems.

"Because of budget problems, our department isn't fully automated. Calls come in to 911, get routed to fire stations, and they respond. Papers don't always get completed or filled out. Firefighters race from call to call. Public safety is our top priority, and sometimes, it means we get behind on the paperwork for it."

That didn't seem like an issue, Lars thought, turning away. He had his own problems. While Srepska had perfected the art of stealthily conducting computer financial crimes, Lars had managed to figure that the bank and its CEO were their pawns. He pondered what else he could figure out. He took his tablet computer over to the chair where the CEO was chained. He ordered Pierce to help him gain access to Srepska's main transaction account at CityFargo. Naturally, the CEO was at his command and did what he asked.

After logging in, Lars could see regular transfers into the account from an offshore account, which he presumed was a front account used by Srepska. He looked down the list of transactions over the last sixty days. Many were high dollar transfers into the account and out of the account. But one stuck out to him: a $250,000 transfer to an industrial vehicle dealership in rural Virginia.

He googled the firm. The dealership sold fire trucks among other commercial vehicles.

A light bulb went off in his mind: *could Srepska have been behind the flooding of the Treasury Department?* he wondered.

Meanwhile, CityFargo had reported to the police that their

CEO was missing, and the news media was speculating whether he was in hiding, afraid to face the wrath of the public. Or, maybe he had been held hostage by the forces behind the current financial crisis. CityFargo insisted that security tape footage appeared to show him disappearing with a tall stranger with a mustache and dark hair. They speculated that it could possibly be a kidnapper, although it appeared the CEO was leaving on his own free will without any threat of violence.

The parking attendant was interviewed and he relayed the story of how the tall person accompanying the CEO had flashed a badge at him. Lars froze as a police spokesman stated that they were looking for a possible police imposter. *Were my disguise and fake license plate adequate?* he thought. *Of course, they were. Even if the police want to search DMV records for my car, they will never know it is a different color than what is on file at DMV, and will be a different color next time I pull out of my driveway with it. This is exactly why I don't do jobs in the area I live.*

Lars contemplated his next step. He had to go to Philadelphia, but his first step should be covering his back here in Los Angeles. He didn't want to get tripped up at a crucial moment in his investigation by some local cop.

Lars called his girlfriend, Camile Vargas. She was at her office in the Los Angeles County District Attorney's Office branch at the Pasadena Courthouse. She had told Lars that she would be reviewing several case files in advance of a series of sentencing hearings scheduled for the next day on felony criminal cases.

"Can you come home by six tonight?" Lars asked. He did not like asking her to leave early for the day, as he knew that she had a large volume of time-sensitive work to accomplish.

"Sure. Have you seen the news? Everyone's talking about it and doesn't know what to make of it. The judge whose courtroom I had a couple of cases in this afternoon just announced that she was postponing all of her afternoon hearings today until next week."

Lars was still downstairs in the basement, interrogating the CEO when he heard Camile come in, less than an hour after the call.

"What's going on?" she asked as Lars walked up the stairs.

"Let's sit down," Lars said as he pointed to the kitchen table.

When she was settled in, he went on, "Look, I had a job and I think it's a lead to what's going on with this financial crisis. I was hired by my client for the job initially, but I'm on my own here because my client doesn't want any sort of trail to lead to them. We have someone downstairs who might just be able to give us some answers."

"What?" she asked. "Why downstairs?"

This could get tricky, Lars thought. *I should just get to the point.*

"Someone is, shall you say, my guest downstairs. You know how I can do my work anywhere and have all my tools downstairs ready to travel with me anywhere in the world. Well, today I am holding a man here down in the basement so I can extract the information I need from him. He doesn't know where he is. And as you would expect, he thinks I look much different than I really do."

"Are you out of your mind?" she asked. "You promised that you would never do any more jobs in the United States."

Yes, but never did I expect to get paid the sort of money I was offered a job that is right up my alley.

"What you did is crazy. You could go to jail, I could go to jail…"

Another one of these, he thought as he took a deep breath and tried to do his best to look engaged while simultaneously thinking of whether the police would soon be on their way to his house. He wasn't really listening to what she was saying, as he began focusing on how to change the conversation to what he needed to discuss.

"I understand. You are angry because I brought work home. But you know the business I am in," he calmly said.

"This cannot be happening. What have you gotten us into?

You know how I feel about you bringing your work too close to home, and now you have brought your work *in* our home? What you were thinking?"

"Hold on," he said. "You think I like this? The only reason I'm doing this is to help out people. Our country is paralyzed by a bunch of crazy hackers." He paused to let that sink in. At last she nodded reluctantly. "I'm trying to get to the bottom of this situation, and my guest is helping me do that."

After some more back and forth, they both agreed to work together to work through the issue. *This went exactly how I expected,* Lars thought, pleased with himself.

Camile had a friend from law school who now worked for the Justice Department in Dallas. But she was hesitant to call him to make the connection.

Lars clicked the remote in the living room where they were talking. A financial news channel came on the plasma television mounted on the wall. The commentator noted that the U.S. stock market had lost fully five percent for the day. Certain stocks temporarily stopped trading for the day because of their sharp drops. And the stock markets in Asia had lost five percent at the start of trading as a result of the uncertainty in what was suspected to be a computer virus that was impacting the ability of millions of Americans to pay for everyday purchases. Gold had sustained its largest one-day increase in many years.

"I think I am on to something here. I just need your help."

"I don't know that I want to get involved," she said, resisting. "I tell you what," she sighed, "you can use my name and say you are working for me. That happens all the time, when investigators from one jurisdiction call colleagues in another to share information and swap ideas. Call Mika Pavic, an assistant U.S. attorney in Dallas who also leads an organized crime task force. I have his cell-phone number, and I wouldn't be surprised if he were still at the office even though it's after seven o'clock there. Tell him you are working for me, calling him at the suggestion of Patrick Joshi in the FBI, who referred you to him. It's perfectly believable. Patrick is a supervisory special agent who leads our work on counterterrorism cases here, so he probably has heard of him."

Lars got out his phone and called Pavic.

"Have you heard of Srepska?" Lars inquired.

"Excuse me, who are you?"

"I am a DA's investigator out here in California. I am working on a case for Camile Vargas in the DA's office. It's a joint case with the FBI, and Special Agent Joshi in the FBI field office told me to give you a call. My boss is pushing me to make some progress on a big case, and I thought perhaps we could help out each other and share information we have."

There was silence for a few long moments on the phone. Lars wondered whether his ruse would work. *Let's hope he hasn't worked with others in the DA's office and ask me a question about how someone he worked with on a case is doing.*

"Fine. Everything I tell you, you never heard from me. You didn't even talk to me. We are having a hypothetical call about hypothetical things. It won't help your team get a grand jury indictment, but may lead you to information that will, if you know what I mean. Deal?"

"Deal. I never talked to you."

"The answer to your question is yes, of course. We suspect that this gang got millions of dollars in an insider trading deal when they hacked into a large pharmaceutical company's computer network to learn that they were about to be acquired by a larger rival. They then placed stock trades with the information that brought them boatloads of money. And, our friends in Switzerland say that they 'shorted' the stock of a bank—in other words, placing a bet that the stock value would fall, and then starting a false news story that the bank was on the verge of bankruptcy. Those stock trades netted *someone* thousands of dollars."

"Between you and me, do we know who is behind Srepska?" Lars inquired.

"Well, the efforts to track the *who* haven't been so promising because of a maze-like series of financial transactions that makes finding the bad guys really hard. Our agents at Homeland Security and the FBI are frustrated, but they aren't going to give up. We have tried to work with Interpol, but that hasn't helped yet. Did I mention Britain is trying to uncover Srepska's involvement in a large intellectual-property crime ring in the United Kingdom that sells knockoff products? If we ever figure out who they are, we will have to first have a fight to get at the front of the line to prosecute them."

Lars thanked Pavic and concluded the call. *Should I travel to Philadelphia to learn more about the person calling Srepska's U.S. shots or go to Washington, DC, to try to ascertain more about what happened at the Treasury Department?* Lars pondered. *I have a much clearer lead in Philadelphia.*

"I still cannot believe we have someone stashed in our basement," Camile noted in an agitated voice once he hung up. "What if someone finds out? You aren't working abroad like you normally do, where you just fly into a country, track someone down, kill them, make it look like natural causes with all your pharmaceutical tricks, leave the country, and enjoy a large sum of money."

"I am going to go to Philadelphia," Lars said calmly. *I don't really know how she will take this. But do I really care anymore?* he thought. "Don't worry, you will be alone in the house. The man downstairs is coming with me, and no one ever knows he was here, so you don't have to worry at all."

"Philadelphia? Why Philadelphia?"

"I have a lead on where these people I need to find are. The address is in Philadelphia. And if that doesn't pan out, I will be going down to Virginia to learn more about why this outfit purchased fire trucks."

She glanced toward the basement stairs as he continued. "I already found my flight plan. I will just need to stop once—at a non-tower airport in Missouri that has self-service fuel that I can pay for using my Phillips Aviation Fuel card." He had already thought this part through. *This card doesn't work over the regular credit card system, so I should be able to use it. If not, there probably won't be anyone around at the airport at the time I am there, so I can try to bypass the card reader and get fuel anyway,* Lars thought. *If not, I will be stuck in the middle of the country so I can just drive the rest of the way. It would set my plans back, but I would be closer to completion than I am now.*

"And you think you can just fly there now?"

"Are you kidding?" he said, smiling for the first time today. "With the country driven to its knees, I'd like to see somebody try to stop me."

He kissed her goodbye. "Say, why don't you go upstairs so you can honestly say you have no idea of who was in the basement?"

"You don't have to ask me twice."

He went back downstairs, where the banker was slumping in his chair. Probably was passing out from not eating all day. Lars roughly wrapped a cloth around the CEO's eyes, then stuffed a gag in his mouth and secured that too. He loosened the banker's ties. "Don't try anything," he said sharply. "If anything, I'm in a worse mood than I was before." Giving him a hard shove to get his lard ass in gear, he marched him upstairs and into the car.

Lars wasn't taking him back to the bank. He would drop him off on the way. The longer he stayed out of sight, the less Lars would have to worry about him. He stopped on a side street off the Glendale Freeway, and rolled him down a slight hill. Nobody would find him for at least a few hours.

I sure am glad I took the time to earn a pilot's license several years ago. There is no better way to travel than with a private jet, not least because I can carry whatever weapons I need.

He went to Bob Hope Airport in Burbank. He began conducting pre-flight checks on his white Mooney Ovation 3 aircraft with a blue tail. All in all, he thought, a productive day. Scaring a banker out of his wits was fun. Finding clues that would lead him to Pierce's scumbag friends was even better. He waited until he was given clearance by the tower. As the aircraft's engine came to a pre-takeoff roar, he let it taxi forward. He vowed not to come back until he could use his credit card again.

CHAPTER 21

THE NEXT MORNING, Fredric weighed his options. Should I go to Philadelphia on my own and stake out the location Lim gave me? But what if she had listed a fake address? *I would waste valuable time on a wild goose chase. But if it were a valid address, I would have a valuable lead into Srepska's operations here in the states.*

The clock was ticking before the military strikes on Myanmar. Above all else, he had to prevent that from happening. If North Korea or China was dragged into the conflict, all bets were off. Including all bets in the Motherland, he thought glumly.

He got out his phone and called.

"Listen, I've decided what I will do. Srepska's expertise is in cybercrime. That means bread crumbs exist that I can follow. Who's in charge of solving the links of the attack?"

"A National Cyber Investigative Joint Task Force coordinates the federal response. And the FBI leads it. But many others are heavily involved, like Homeland Security and the Secret Service. Probably even the Cybercrimes Command at the Pentagon. And then the financial regulators. Many agencies, is the answer. Homeland Security has said that it is still not clear the attacks are related to terrorism," Lim said.

"Can you set it up for me to pose as an IT expert from the Justice Department? That would give me time to help unravel the current mess," Fredric asked.

"You got it."

"But one thing: don't tell anyone in your Department, tell no one who doesn't know." *Where would be the best place for me to go?* Fredric thought. *Somewhere that is not the central hub of action that would be tightly controlled and everyone probably knows everyone. Where could I go to get access to computer networks and information that would be helpful but that people would not immediately know I am an outsider?* "Let's make that place be the Federal Reserve Board since they have a unique way to see inside the payment system."

Lim replied quickly, "Here's a deal. I know a supervisory special agent in the FBI who is completely trustworthy. He is actually not working for the FBI at the moment because he is on detail to me personally as my confidential assistant. In other words, he is someone who advises me, helps me work through the culture to do my job, and basically helps me on all sorts of things that I need to do but just don't have time to do myself. Well, at least that's the job as I understand it, but I am so new in this job that I haven't really been able to fully use his talents. Still, I have known him for several years. Long before I held this job in fact. The guy is a strict law and order type, he's reliable, gung-ho, and I know he's on the up and up. And since he is on detail to me, he can work quietly and confidentially to help you."

At last this Lim character was showing himself to be useful. "That's fine."

"Okay, how about you meet him at Farragut Square in downtown DC? It is two blocks north of the White House at the intersection of K and 17th Streets Northwest. Can you find it or do you need directions?"

"Yes, I can find it easily. I can probably be there in about sixty minutes. Can your guy be ready by then?"

"Knowing Sam, he could still be at the gym this time in the morning so he may be in workout clothes, but I know Sam and I know he will come through. Look for a Chevy Suburban SUV with a yellow piece of paper under the driver's side windshield wiper."

"Deal."

Fredric began biking back toward DC instead of going to the airport. He was getting to like this bike trail, the rolling Virginia countryside. No wonder that it was home to America's founding fathers.

After a hard, satisfying ride, he reached the corner of 17th and K Street and found Farragut Square. *Wow. If my watch is right, I made this trip in forty-five minutes. I made really good time.* He was very pleased with himself. That was the way to make the day start right.

As he got off his bike, he saw that all the benches were occupied by unshaven men in scraggly clothes. Shopping carts filled with assorted junk waited nearby. *What is that guy yelling at?* he thought as someone with a long beard got up off a bench, grabbed his trash bag, and began shouting and pointing at random objects along the sidewalk. *What a mess,* he thought. *They permit these shameful conditions in the nation's capital?*

Fredric leaned his bike next to a fence, sat down on the now unoccupied bench, and took a sip of water. He scanned the perimeter of the park, which took up a full city block. He noticed that it was only possible to park on one side of the park as the other sides were busy streets. *I bet the traffic is much lighter today than a normal weekday morning, given the financial turmoil,* he thought.

After twenty minutes of waiting, he saw a black Chevy Suburban pull up to the head of the block. *I suspect this is who I am waiting to see,* he pondered as he stared at the heavily tinted passenger side windows. He would avoid staring or doing anything out of the ordinary until he could better assess whether this vehicle was alone or if there were others. A guy in his early forties got out of the driver's side and slipped a piece of yellow paper on the passenger's side windshield wiper. He figured this was Sam.

He walked his bike over toward the SUV. The driver's window went down. Inside, he saw a CB radio and a placard in the window indicating that the vehicle was a federal law enforcement vehicle on official business. Then he spotted a set of red lights mounted below the rearview mirror.

Fredric approached the window and asked, "Are you Sam?" *I don't see anyone else in the back seat.*

"Yes, sir. You must be Fredric. Let me take care of your bike," the driver said as he got out of the vehicle and walked around to open the back door. He folded the rear passenger seats down, and Fredric laid his bike down in the back.

Sam gave Fredric a long once-over, taking in his getup. "Sir, we will both look a lot more credible where we are going if we get you into some business casual clothes before we go. Your face and clothes look scraggly like a street person. No need for a suit since we are law enforcement, just something a little more suitable for a professional environment. I have something you can wear. How about you change in the back of the car?"

As Sam was driving to the Federal Reserve building, Fredric changed into tan Dockers and a gray shirt. They were a size too big but nothing that was noticeable.

"You were in the Army?" Fredric asked Sam on the way as he noticed a sticker in the rear door's window.

"Proud Army veteran. I worked counterintelligence."

Fredric was pleased to learn this. "I served for five years in the Bundeswehr—that's the German federal defense forces. I saw combat in Afghanistan. My best friend was killed by an IED south of Kabul," he added quietly. "He was a gunner on top of our Humvee when we were attacked. To this day I'm haunted by how he died so suddenly and the rest of us were untouched."

"I lost a few buddies myself," Sam said, shaking his head. "Those memories, they don't go away."

They soon realized that they had both served in Afghanistan

during the same time frame, although they were in different parts of the country so they likely had never crossed paths. Fredric began thinking how he had been stationed in south Berlin when the Berlin Wall came down in 1989. Sam mentioned that he was a senior in high school at that time and already talking with a recruiter about entering the military after graduation.

Sam soon parked on a side street near the entrance of the Federal Reserve Building. He flashed his badge and the card on his dashboard to the guard.

Fredric opened his door and stepped out. He looked up and noticed several security cameras that were monitoring all directions. Two guards were standing outside carrying assault rifles around their shoulders. He also noticed infrared motion detectors designed to detect any movement around the perimeter.

It would not be possible to enter this building any other way. But then he chuckled to himself. *How else could I walk through the front door wearing a blue windbreaker with FBI on the back?*

"Let me take the lead on talking to them," Sam said. "I can detect your German accent. Let's not unnecessarily give anyone a reason to strike up a conversation with us that can get us off track or call your identity into question."

Sam flashed his FBI credentials to the Federal Reserve guards as they entered. "My partner Franklin Ryder is with me. We are here to see the Chief of Staff." As they agreed earlier, Fredric quickly flashed an FBI ID case with badge as he was talking.

They were quickly ushered through the high-security doors to an elevator lobby. From there a guard escorted them to a large conference room. "He will be here shortly," the guard said as he walked off.

No one looks like they are in charge or is clear on what they are doing, Fredric thought as he scanned the conference room. All the people sitting around were either on laptops, talking on cellphones, or checking blackberries. *Everyone looks puzzled or worried.*

A man in a suit walked over to them. "I am the Deputy Chief of Staff of the Federal Reserve," the man said. "The attorney general called my boss and said that he was going to be sending in one of his FBI agents and another expert investigator. He said one of you was a little unconventional but was the absolute best," he added with a chuckle.

The Deputy proceeded to spend five minutes explaining what was going on around them. "Examiners from the Federal Reserve System and investigators from the FBI are probing each of the large payment networks. They are sorting through what's happening. The central computers at the payment processors went offline and no one has been able to reactivate them. These computers are necessary to operate the networks. Backup sites are similarly useless."

"What do you know about the source of the problems?" Sam asked.

"We don't know if the problems were caused by the same source, or whether each problem is independent. Or whether the problem that started with one payment network resulted in increased demand for other payment networks, and the increased stress on those networks taxed their capacity and knocked them off line. But then again, we are relying heavily on the FBI and Department of Homeland Security. I am told that the Department of Defense's Cybercrime Command thinks that the attacks originated from Myanmar." He shook his head slightly at that preposterous idea. "It is too early to know more. I tell you, I never thought I would be in the middle of a case involving a sophisticated international crime ring."

"Do we think that they have gradually introduced malware into key computer systems to pave the way, to whatever it is that they are planning?" Fredric asked.

"There's no way to be sure, at least not at this moment."

Fredric asked to review network traffic logs for incoming internet traffic to the key processing centers for each of the four key payment networks. "I don't know what I'll be able to spot, but that seems like a good place to start."

Shortly after making the request, Federal Reserve staff gave Fredric and Sam a laptop with downloads of network traffic logs over the past six months. These showed the IP address of the computers that accessed the computer systems for the key corporate computer networks for VISA, MasterCard, Discover, and American Express. The logs were lengthy and would take days, perhaps weeks or even months, to review. *I have a hunch that whoever we are after logged into these networks to exploit their hidden doors. They must have launched the attack around the time that I was in Budapest. That would link up with what I was hearing back in the hotel while listening into the calls from Srepska's safe house,* he thought.

That narrowed down the timeframe to about a week. *Even so, how am I going to sort through all these leads when the clock is ticking?*

He knew that anyone who accessed the internet would have been assigned a user ID, known as an IP address. It represented the computer or other device the person used. This IP address was transferred with everything that they transmitted or received on the internet. In other words, when someone visited or otherwise accessed a website, a unique ID—one that in theory was traceable back to the computer that the person surfing the web was using—was transmitted along with their request.

The IP address connected to a problem, in theory, could be tracked back to its source. But identifying the genuine IP address might be a problem because it could have been faked, forged, or otherwise concealed. Still, though, even when the legitimate IP address was not available, the style of coding, encryption used, and regular access from a single source could be valuable clues.

Fredric exported the files into a spreadsheet. He decided to cross-reference the remaining IP addresses to identify any that had logged into all three networks within a two-hour period.

After a few keystrokes to build and run a database query,

he found an IP address. "I need you to find what computer this belongs to," he asked Sam while handing over a piece of paper. *This is a shot in the dark, but it is my best attempt.*

Sam took out his phone. "I need a trace through the internet service provider to find out who and what address is associated with this IP address."

After several long moments, Sam began writing an address on his notepad: 2435 South Street in Philadelphia.

Fredric froze in shock. *Is what I am reading right?* "2435 South Street, Philadelphia?" Fredric asked as his eyes got wide.

"Yes, does that address mean something to you?" was Sam's response.

Fredric confided in Sam the incident involving the Attorney General's intern. "This was her address as well. Either this is a made-up address they are using, or it is a building where they have ties and connections. Either way, it is our best hope to find someone who can lead us to the people we are after," Fredric told Sam in a hushed voice.

Sam and Fredric conferred on what to do. Sam wanted to call the FBI's Philadelphia field office and coordinate obtaining a search warrant from the local on-duty U.S. magistrate authorizing an immediate search of the premises located at 2435 South Street.

Sam said, "We have the expertise and equipment to take this from here. You have done us a tremendous service. But the FBI will handle it from this point. Attorney General Lim will be very grateful for your help and service."

But Fredric was not so trusting. "It's not safe to communicate what we are doing within the Justice Department," he argued, "because we don't know to what degree Srepska has assets working within the FBI. In fact, there is a known Srepska asset within the Attorney General's inner circle, and while he knows it, he cannot do anything about it right now."

Sam paused to consider a possible breach. "Understood. You

are right, ultimately I am working for Lim, and he was clear that I was to assist you. So, what exactly do you suggest we do? We could go to the address and secure the location ourselves." He didn't seem to like this option, and stated a qualifier. "But you have to agree that I bring in the FBI at the point in time when we really are sure that we are dealing with the people who caused these problems."

This guy is starting to think like I do. "Deal," Fredric said, even as another thought occurred to him. *I hope he doesn't update the other people in his office on where he and I are going.*

Sam got out his phone and placed a call. "I am pursuing a lead that will take me the rest of the day. Won't be back in today."

"It's that easy?" Fredric asked.

"I have a great boss. He trusts me and I am in a position where I work fairly independently. He just wants me to get the job done and do things the right way. You want to go now?" Sam asked.

"Yes. Let's—how do you say it?—put the pedal to the metal."

Sam laughed and clapped Fredric on the shoulder. "Yes, that's how we say it. What do you say we hightail it to Philly?"

Fredric liked the sound of that, like an American Western movie. What he liked even more was the repeated use of the same address. Anyone with a grain of sense knew better than to believe in coincidences.

CHAPTER 22

IN THE UNDERGROUND bunker at the White House, the presidential impersonator was doing his best to stay still in his chair. If he stood up and started pacing, trying to work off his anxiety, his upper body would be seen by the security cameras. More to the point, his face would be seen. He looked enough like the President to pass, as long as the look was fleeting. Anyone who watched him too long, though, might start to notice the subtle differences. He would be found out and then what? He was trapped inside one of the most heavily guarded buildings in the world.

Fat chance I'd ever get away, he thought. Not for the first time, it occurred to him that Zoltan had never thought he would get out. *I was such a fool, letting him talk me into this.* He was a graduate of the University of Szeged, after all, the highest institute of learning in all of Hungary. That's why he was chosen for this role. He was smart enough to pull off such a stunt. He was too tempted by the money Zoltan kept whispering in his ear. *You'll be a millionaire. You'll never have to work again.* That was such a lie, he could see that now.

He reached for the box of Kleenex on the table. Next to it was a pile of used tissues—used not to blow his nose but to wipe the sweat off his face. The room was so hot. He hadn't noticed it when he first entered, but by now he was sweltering. Didn't they know how to keep their presidents in comfort?

He glanced at the false Secret Service officers seated on either side of him. They hadn't attended university. They were hoodlums hired off the streets of Joseph Town, the worst slum in the city. Underneath their dapper blazers, they carried Walther PPKs. He knew that they had been trained to shoot their way out if things went wrong. The thought of it made him nervous all over again. He didn't even like guns. How in the world had he ended up here?

The screen of the laptop in front of him suddenly glowed. The program it was running was Srepska's version of a VOIP line, secure from anyone who might want to listen in. In the window appeared the face of the person he least wanted to see at this moment.

Zoltan did not look good. His long white hair was unkempt, like he'd run his hand through it too many times. "Gergely," he snapped, "put on your headset, you dolt. What are you thinking?"

Frightened, Gergely immediately reached for the Sennheiser headphones lying next to the computer. He jammed them on so quickly, the rubber pads scraped the tops of his ears.

"So," Zoltan continued, "how is it going there? You have set forth the order about Myanmar, I see. Has anyone consulted you about further moves?"

"No, so far—"

"You idiot! Everyone there can hear you. Just answer yes or no, like we discussed!"

"No." Gergely noticed that his hands were trembling wildly on the tabletop. He quickly shoved them into his lap to calm them down.

"All right," Zoltan said in more measured tones. "Everything is going well otherwise. The Americans are still scrambling, trying to find out how their financial system went haywire." The older man could not hide a smile of satisfaction. "You just keep calm. When the time comes, we'll be extracting you. We also have a back door into the security system at the White House, as we talked about before. It will go haywire and you will be able to escape in the confusion." The leathery face grew stern. "Do you understand?"

"Yes, Zol—"

"Just yes or no!"

"Y-yes. Ah, that's an affirmative."

Zoltan disappeared from the screen, and Gergely nearly collapsed in his seat. He just had to maintain the fiction for a while longer. The money would be siphoned off soon, and he wouldn't be needed any longer.

At least that is what he kept telling himself.

CHAPTER 23

EARLIER THAT MORNING, Lars had risen after sleeping on the airplane that was parked in a private airfield. *It's already 8:00 a.m.,* he thought. That was late enough to call a former Canadian client. Justin Fairfield had, during the month Lars worked for him, rising every morning at five o'clock sharp.

"Justin, it's Lars. How are things?"

After a few remarks about how long it had been, Lars jumped to what was on his mind. "What's up with the U.S. about to attack Burma? Come on, Burma waging war on the most powerful nation in the world? This new president must be getting some bad advice about their acting as a front for China and North Korea. Why would anyone believe this? Everyone knows it would be economic suicide for them to do this. Do you have any inside dope about what is happening?"

Justin laughed. "Burma is merely the fall guy for the problems caused by someone—or something—else. The wool is probably being pulled over the government's eyes by a sophisticated network of computer hackers. Think of it this way: we all feared something like this would happen someday." There was a pause, and when Justin spoke again, the tone of his voice was more questioning. "But there is of course another possibility too. This is being used as an excuse by the U.S. government to attack Burma for some other reason, a reason that they are not at liberty to disclose to the public."

That could possibly make sense, Lars thought. "Or at least not ready to tell the public just yet," he said aloud. "Okay, thanks. Makes sense. Let's keep in touch."

He walked a light Zero motorcycle he'd secured in the plane's center aisle out the cockpit door and set it upright on the runway. *How did the yellow paint get scratched?* he thought. It was right on the fuel tank, right where he'd see it every time he got on the chopper.

Dismissing his annoyance, he revved it up and took off. He'd landed in a private airport called Wings Field, northeast of the city, and he wended his way from the suburbs into downtown Philadelphia. He passed the expansive green swath anchored by the Philadelphia Museum before his GPS told him he was getting close.

This is South Street… and that house says 2435. He noticed that the address appeared to be a two-story brick residential house that was probably fifty years old.

He parked the motorcycle down the block. The blinds covering the windows of the house looked very clean, like cheap blinds that could be quickly put up to cover windows, he thought. They covered every inch of glass very well. As he walked past the home, he noticed that the electric meter was turning rather rapidly. What inside is using so much electricity?

The answer came to him immediately: anyone using a lot of servers for computers.

Lars noticed that a minivan was parked in front of the house, but again he realized that the vehicle could belong to anyone on the block and not necessarily have a connection to 2435 South Street. But the hood of the car felt lukewarm as if it had been moved within the past hour or so.

He needed a ruse to find out if anyone was home. He used his tablet computer to place an order for a pizza that would be delivered to the house. He entered his credit card number to pay for the pizza online, but he got an error message saying *transaction refused.* Of course, the financial network was down. He went back into the order and changed it to pay on delivery. He planned to watch carefully to see if anyone answered the door when the delivery came, and if so, who it was.

About thirty minutes later, a car with a pizza delivery sign on top pulled up near the house. *The website said they delivered within twenty minutes,* he noted with slight annoyance. The delivery person knocked and rang the bell.

After waiting, the driver rang the bell again and knocked on the door. The driver looked at his order slip and then up at the 2435 number hanging above the door. This time, he heard the knocking from where he was waiting halfway down the street. Lars then saw him take the pizza back into his car and drive away.

Fifteen minutes later, Lars saw a short man leave the house and get into a white Ford Taurus parked halfway up the block. *That barcode sticker on the rear passenger window and its clean, shiny appearance tells me that it has to be a rental car.*

He had to decide whether to stay at the house or follow this car. He had thought the house was connected to Srepska based on the information he had obtained back in Los Angeles, but then the thought crossed his mind: *what if they already cleared out at this address? What if the bank CEO told his Hungarian buddies what happened?*

He got on his motorcycle and revved it up. He waited until the car drove a couple blocks before he started to follow it.

The car drove through the streets of Philadelphia, onto the interstate. The car then drove about twenty miles south and took an exit that appeared to have little more than a gas station, truck stop, and a host of industrial buildings. He followed from a safe distance as the car drove four miles on wide streets with retreaded tires and other debris on the sides of the streets, along with plenty of gravel. These streets were built for and primarily used by semi-trucks. Lars was careful to stay far back to avoid being visible. He saw the car turn off in front of a warehouse building that had nothing other than the street number printed on the front of the business. It was next to a distribution center for a snack food company, and nearby was the freight terminal for an overnight package delivery company.

He took out his phone and bookmarked his exact location. He began to head back to the 2435 South Street house and see what was inside the house before he risked driving up to the warehouse, where he easily could be outnumbered.

By the time he returned to the house in Philadelphia, it was almost noon.

He parked his motorcycle a block away and walked to the house. He knocked on the door. But no one answered. *The time is now,* he thought as he could feel his heart racing with a sudden rush of adrenaline. He walked to a side door, down a narrow alley that smelled of years of garbage. He opened his backpack and removed a tool. He used the automated lock pick to unlock the door. He pulled his M&P22 pistol out of the holder on his waistband, which had been hidden by a long leather jacket. He carefully screwed on the suppressor. *I need to get in and out before the guy I saw comes back.*

He entered the house quietly. He walked through a galley kitchen and into a main room that was empty. No furniture, no nothing. Yet the room temperature was a warm seventy degrees. *So why would the electric meter be moving so fast?* he thought. *Clearly there must be something somewhere in this house that is draining it.*

He cautiously walked through the house. Every room he went into was empty. *I was pretty good at guessing what they eat here,* he thought as he saw an open but empty pizza box in what must be a bedroom.

Why would someone be using the house when there is nothing in it? Lars wondered.

He had returned to the main room downstairs when he heard what sounded like the hum of fans coming from a stairwell to the basement. The door to the stairwell was open.

He noticed that a light was on downstairs. Still, even as he crept up to the doorway, he couldn't see much downstairs. He smelled cigarette smoke. It could have been remnants from the person who had left about an hour earlier. But it seemed very strong to him. He could see windows at the base of the stairs and noticed that they were sealed. *Why would they seal the windows?*

He decided that he would venture downstairs cautiously, with his gun drawn.

As he softly took a couple steps down, a tableau of a young man holding a tablet computer came into view. Sure enough, he was smoking a cigarette. The man was seated in front of two computer server racks that stood seven feet tall and five feet wide. What appeared to be an AK-47 assault rifle was propped up next to the chair.

His suspicions were confirmed. This was a Srepska outpost. Why else would there be the computer equipment guarded by a man with a heavy-duty firearm? He thought back to why he was there: the German BND had contracted with him to find and neutralize Srepska operations in the United States, wherever they might be. He thought about the current chaos: no one being able to make a purchase with cash and generally unable to get cash from ATMs, and the fact that the US was about to attack Myanmar.

He was not sure what to do. On the one hand, should he try to capture the guy and find out what he knows, or should he just shoot him? The computers no doubt contained tons of data, and he might need the passwords.

Then Lars saw that the man had a small black handgun in his other hand. This guy had to be a thug, not a programmer. At any moment he could turn around and notice Lars bent over on the stairs.

As though his thought had been transmitted, the man suddenly swiveled in his chair. Seeing Lars, he shouted in alarm. He was raising his gun when Lars, firmly holding his M&P22 in both hands, fired a silenced shot. The man's forehead grew an angry third eye, and his body was thrown violently off the chair, which spun wildly across the cement floor. *I guess that takes care of the Q and A session,* he thought grimly.

Holding the gun ready to fire, to take out anyone he hadn't seen, Lars continued to walk down the stairs. He went to a Surface notebook computer at a table near the computer servers. Around it there were several folding chairs. The only noise he heard was the quiet humming of the servers. Bending down over the sprawled body, he checked the pockets and pulled out his wallet and cellphone. He placed the cellphone on the table as he emptied the contents of the wallet. It had several $50 and $100 bills and a Pennsylvania driver's license. He picked through the wallet and found several cards and papers that appeared to be written in an Eastern European language. *I will have to brush up on my Hungarian.*

He picked up the phone, and when the screen illuminated, he saw that it required a password. He entered 1234. That was not it. Then he entered the four-digit street number of the house. Again, it would not unlock. Lars tossed it back on the table. *Of course, it wouldn't be that easy.* He carefully reviewed the notebook's desktop, but besides the familiar icons, all the files were titled with the same inscrutable language. *I am going to need a translator to read anything in here.*

He glanced up suddenly. There was a webcam on one of the computers. It seemed to be pointing toward the stairwell. He quickly turned it sideways so that no one would be able to see what was happening.

Was anyone watching what just happened?

He had to get out of there, pronto. Whoever drove that car to the warehouse would drive back if he was alerted to any trouble. Like an assassin invading their basement.

Working quickly but methodically, Lars grabbed the Surface and stuffed it into a tote case parked conveniently against one of the legs of the table. The FBI could figure out what was on it. He had a fleeting thought of shooting all the servers, taking them out of the game, but he held back. Maybe they didn't see him. In that case, there was no point alerting them by having a bank of servers going offline.

Grabbing the case, Lars took a last look around. What was this place? Was it an outpost, or was it a vital center? He didn't know, but at least he had learned something valuable.

Srepska was no figment of the imagination. It was alive and well in the U.S.A.

CHAPTER 24

MEANWHILE, FREDRIC AND Sam were driving up I-95 when they began to see the skyline. The address we are going to can't be far away, Fredric thought as he saw signs for the Philadelphia airport.

Using his hands-free phone, Sam called the Philadelphia FBI field office and spoke to his counterpart, the special agent in charge. He explained that he was on an active investigation on a matter that originated from his territory and might need their assistance soon. "This is standard operating protocol for when an agent based in one field office works in the geographic jurisdiction of another field office," he explained to Fredric.

They got off at the Ben Franklin Bridge and worked their way west, past the city center, until they arrived at their destination, 2435 South Street. They got out and walked around. Fredric noticed the side alley almost immediately, and when they walked around back, he could tell that someone had fiddled with the lock and got in the back door. The lock cylinder where someone would normally put their key was turned sideways. Sam grabbed a glove from his pocket and turned the handle. The door opened.

Fredric turned to Sam and asked, "This is your call. Should we both go in?"

"Normally I would have to call a judge to get a warrant. But we have an exigent circumstance here—there was a break-in of a house." He cracked a slight smile, and Fredric realized he was making up an excuse. "So I can go in because I have reason to believe a crime is in progress and the resident of the house could be in imminent danger. But I should make you wait outside."

"But we didn't come all this way for me to shoot the breeze while you do all the hard work."

"Why don't you wait outside," Sam said with a smirk. "But trust me, if you follow me in, I have much higher priorities right now than to arrest you for trespassing or interfering with a federal investigation."

Sam pushed open the door with his foot. He had his standard-issue FBI service revolver drawn, a Glock 23. Fredric drew his own gun and waved toward the downstairs. Sam lined up behind him as if to cover him in the event of a firefight. Fredric was holding an ultra-compact handgun that resembled a Rohrbaugh R9 but was made out of hard plastic.

"You call that a gun?" Sam quietly whispered, trying to avoid laughter. "That's what a child might use for self-defense. You call yourself an intelligence operative with that? Or is that what you Europeans call an assault rifle," Sam whispered while chuckling quietly.

"Works perfectly every time," Fredric said, ignoring the attempt at humor. "I cannot just board an airplane with a gun like you can, I imagine, much less get through Customs to enter the country. You adapt to your environment and work with what you got."

"Point taken. Okay, let's do this," Sam said as he stepped through the door from the back vestibule.

Together they scanned the first room. Fredric thought, *The fact that the sofa is the only piece of furniture in this room is a solid clue that this isn't a regular residential house.*

The next room was empty too except for a recliner.

Fredric held his breath as he smelled a rotten smell from the kitchen. *Disgusting. Whoever is working out of this house must not care to clean it.* He glanced around the kitchen and saw only a small brown rectangular table with folding chairs. *More appropriate for a break room than a kitchen.*

He then saw a door open to a downstairs basement. The light was on. Fredric pointed with his gun down to Sam. "Maybe our friends are down there," he whispered.

Fredric walked down the stairs first, followed by Sam.

Lars was at the table going through the phone of the dead agent.

Fredric saw the body first. Sam saw Lars first.

"Freeze, I'm FBI. Show me your hands!"

Lars dropped the phone, turned around, saw the FBI windbreakers, and dropped his gun. He slowly put his hands up.

"Get down on the ground," Sam said.

Fredric noticed the assault rifle near the person who was shot. *Something is not right here,* he thought. "Wait, tell us why you are here," he said.

"I am an investigator from Los Angeles, and I am tracking a criminal ring that has international connections. I am on a special assignment, and I'm not authorized to speak about it."

Fredric and Sam looked at each other with disbelief as if to say, *Is this guy for real?*

Fredric spoke up, "My partner is a federal agent with a top security clearance. I myself am working on a case involving an Eastern European crime ring. You better start telling us what you're doing here. We came specifically to this address for a reason, and you are our suspect until you convince us otherwise."

Sam joined in with a hard voice, "You had better start talking fast or we are going to arrest you and you will spend the rest of your life in prison."

Lars didn't look like he was entirely convinced, and he said, "Somebody is going to have to show me some official hardware."

Sam nodded, seeing the sense in that request. Keeping his gun held steady, he used his left hand to flick open his jacket and reveal his FBI badge. "Satisfied."

Lars was about to come closer, but Fredric waved for him to stay put.

Lars peered at the badge from where he was, then shrugged. "Okay, I am on official business to track a crime syndicate called Srepska. I have reason to believe that this house is being used by them as part of their conspiracy to wreak chaos in the U.S. The guy on the floor is part of their racket. Now tell me who you are and what you are after."

Fredric was stunned to find out that this nameless person was after the same gang he was. Still, Lars looked like he meant business wherever he went. Whatever he did, he had the cold-eyed stare of a stone killer.

"As you might have noticed from my accent, I am German. I am working for my employer to find the leaders of Srepska and neutralize them. But who sent you and why?" Fredric sized up the man in front of him. *Why is he wearing quality rimless eyeglasses and expensive leather shoes? Plus, that tan. He must spend a lot of time on the beach in some sunny part of the world.*

"I am an independent contractor, but I won't ever say who I am working for on this job. Even if you were holding hot coals over my body, I wouldn't utter a word about who hired me. Let's just say, we both want to eliminate Srepska, and I have some information that I think we both could work together on."

"OK, let's talk. I am Fredric and this is Sam. How about we talk about this with all of our guns put away?" he said as he leaned down to replace his gun in his ankle holster. He then extended his right hand toward Lars. "Now you. Put that thing away."

Lars nodded, though his face showed his continuing mistrust.

Sam was still holding his gun, but his body and face had a frozen appearance. He was battling conflicting emotions.

"Sam, lighten up," Fredric said with a laugh. "If beach boy here wants to draw, he still is facing two of us."

Slowly, Sam's right arm lowered to the side of his belt. He holstered his firearm, but his hand stayed on the butt.

"I am Special Agent Davis, FBI, Washington."

Lars and Sam shook hands.

"I assumed that I was working alone," said Fredric. Trying to catch Lars off guard, he fired off in rapid-fire German, "Who are you? Who do you work for?"

Lars gave him a perplexed look. "Sorry, I don't know German. You were doing pretty well in English before."

For Fredric, he had passed one test. *I guess this guy isn't working for BND too. Who knows how many people are on the same trail I am on?* Fredric thought.

"OK, here is what I know," Lars said, taking control of the situation. "Srepska has used a bank out in Los Angeles named City-Fargo Bank to launder money and conduct financial operations. The CEO of the bank is their water boy. Don't ask me how I did it, but I tracked the people from Srepska he deals with to this address. I just got here from Southern California in the wee hours of the morning. Before I came inside, I followed someone who left the house. I tailed them to a small warehouse about half an hour from here. I think we should all go there—I think that may be their base of operations in this country. It is out in the countryside, not a lot around other than some warehouses and industrial buildings. There were several cars outside. I saw a small satellite dish that is probably being used for internet connectivity and phone communications," Lars continued.

What he said rang true with Fredric. Southern California sure answered his question about the guy's tan. He said, "They are a lot more powerful than you probably realize. I think they are responsible for the massive payment system problems that have paralyzed the country. They have managed to infiltrate someone into the

U.S. government to blackmail the attorney general." Lars blinked in surprise, and Fredric nodded. "Even your president is somehow being fooled by them to want to wage war on Myanmar. Srepska could be using these very servers to frame Myanmar," he said as he pointed around the room.

Sam spoke up. "This house looks very promising. Let me call the Philadelphia field office. Within an hour, we can have cyber-crime and forensic experts crawling over this place, and they can not only figure out what is happening but who else is involved and what we need to do to stop it."

"Not such a good idea," Fredric said. "If they infiltrated the attorney general's office, how do we know that they haven't compromised the FBI here as well? I have no doubt that practically everyone you work with is honest and all that, but all it takes is one person blackmailed by Srepska who has access to electronic communications and is able to find out what is going on and feed it back to Hungary. Remember, their hacking skills are second to none."

Lars blinked at this mention of a new link, and he asked, "Hungary?"

"That's where I was investigating before I came here," Fredric replied. "Since Srepska goons tried to kill me twice, I would guess I got a little too close for their liking."

Fredric then began thinking through how he would find a list of the types of third-party companies that major banks in Europe would likely rely on to perform key operations. He thought of technology service providers that enable people to use their credit cards, banks to transmit electronic check images, and banks to transfer money to one another to make financial transactions possible. He figured that he could get help to build out the list with specific company names later on.

"I didn't come all the way from sunny Southern California to Pennsylvania in the middle of January to suddenly need help," Lars said sharply. "If you guys want to join forces, I can see that, but

I'm not sitting around this basement for long. I propose that we mine these computer servers for information. I don't know about you, but I'm ready to get started."

Lars walked over to the computer and pulled up a chair. "Fredric, maybe you can see what you can figure out in the phone of this scumbag. By the way, if you haven't guessed already, I had to shoot him." He tossed the phone to Fredric. "At least if you are good with hacking password-protected phones. It can be done, I just don't have the time or software tool to do it with me here."

Fredric put the phone on the table. "I'm not a password cracker either. But I'd sure like to take a look at what they have on this computer." He sat down in front of it and tapped its touch-pad. In another few seconds the screen booted up out of sleep.

"All right," Lars said, not to be outdone. He grabbed the phone back and started tapping in a series of four numbers.

Sam stood motionless but seemed resigned to investigating on their own hook. "Geez, you guys." Sam went to the dead man's coat and put his hand inside the pockets. He then patted down the jeans pockets. He then felt around the ankles. He was soon holding another handgun and what appeared to be a disposable prepaid cellphone.

"Look what I found," he said, but Lars and Fredric were both too busy to do anything but give him a half-hearted glance.

Sam started to go through the phone while Lars and Fredric worked on their tasks.

After a few minutes of the two men silently working in the basement, Sam let out a groan. "I don't think this phone I found on him has been used yet."

"Whoa, I cracked it," Lars said, looking up with a smile. "Most of the codes start with zero, and I tried variations of zero something, zero something. It turns out to be 0-6-0-3. Maybe his wife's birthday."

"Look here," Fredric said as he pointed at the computer. "This computer has been used to log in as an administrator to the two key third-party payment processing systems. These are the backbones for the banks that issue every major debit and credit card. No one has heard of these companies, but they are sure going to by the time all this is over," Fredric said with a quip. "Plus, I see that this computer had logged into the regional transmission organization responsible for moving electricity in the Midwest."

"Oh great, maybe I should call my colleagues in Chicago," Sam remarked sarcastically.

In the meantime, Lars had been furiously manipulating the phone's apps. "Can we see what is happening? I see this phone has been used to call international numbers, a number with a country code of 36," Lars explained. "But there is one number that has the most volume of calls, and it is a local number. And, I found in the online mapping software directions to an address that is probably the warehouse that I was telling you about earlier."

"What country has the country code of 36?" Sam asked.

"That's Hungary," Fredric said.

Lars then pointed all around them. "What do you think all these servers are for? They could be redirecting traffic here, or using this as the hub for all their operations. That means we have a real problem. The three of us trying to undo what they did or even unplugging this equipment could create irrecoverable harm to these companies and just make things worse. They could even have booby-trapped these computers to release lethal instructions across the internet. I know enough to know that the three of us working on the outside need to be really careful or we could cause more damage than where we were to start with."

"You are right, Lars," Fredric responded. "We need to tread carefully here. We are in the middle of a hornet's nest. I know a lot about cyber-warfare and defenses, but I don't have the tools and resources I need to be able to unwind this mess in a way that is risk-free in just a few minutes."

"I have an idea," Sam said. "If what you said is really true and the attorney general is being blackmailed by Srepska, then he has every incentive to be on our side. He wants us to be successful. Let's call him and tell him what's going on and get his advice how to proceed."

"Do you really think you can just call him?" Lars asked incredulously.

"I have friends in high places," he replied.

"Ok, then the next question is: do you trust him?" Lars asked.

"Yes, I do, Lars," Fredric said. "We wouldn't be in this mess if he weren't being blackmailed. You see, I originally brought him the intel. I really believe he feels guilty about what's going on and will help us."

"But I think it's a bit premature. Let's check out what else is in this house," Lars remarked.

Just then they heard a brief chirping sound upstairs.

"Is that a phone?" Fredric asked.

"Maybe the doorbell," Lars said. "It stopped."

"I think we have visitors," Sam said while drawing his gun.

He swiftly moved to a place right underneath the stairs, where he could see through the risers, but someone coming down wouldn't see him. Lars and Fredric dragged the body of the person who was shot out of view. While Lars took up a position to the left of the stairs, Fredric chose to stand in between the racks of servers.

"Hullo!" cried a voice that sounded close, right at the top of the stairs. "Benedek?"

No answer was forthcoming, and they heard the creak of a shoe coming down the first step. Fredric checked the position of Sam and Lars, making sure they couldn't hit each other in a cross fire.

More steps were taken. "Benedek? Are you down there?"

Fredric pointed his gun barrel into an opening above a server at eye level. All he needed was enough of the intruder's body in sight before he fired.

The newcomer hurried down the rest of the stairs. "Benedek, why don't you answer me?"

Fredric could see that the man was armed, holding a pistol at readiness next to his side.

Lars suddenly emerged into view. His firearm was fully extended in the two-handed position. "Okay, asshole, why don't you drop that gun?"

The next moments passed in a blur. The newcomer tried to bring up his gun, and the basement exploded with the chatter of three guns firing at once. The man's chest was peppered with bullets, causing a series of rips across his chest. He groaned loudly as he toppled to the cement floor. His pistol—it was a Glock 23—clattered as it bounced away from the unmoving body. Already his shirt was filling with a swamp of blood.

Lars scowled at the prone body. "Seems like Benedek's friend should have been more cautious."

Fredric emerged from his position of hiding. "That didn't go so well," he remarked as he drew near to Lars, who gave the body a kick to make sure the man was truly dead.

"How's that?" Lars asked.

"I wanted to ask him some questions. Plus, now that we've told the entire neighborhood we're here, we have to leave immediately."

Lars didn't seem fazed by either problem. "Jerk like that, racked and loaded, he wasn't giving up anything."

"No, I suppose not."

Sam joined them. He gave the inert body a frightened glance, then headed up the stairs. "Come on, you two, Fredric was right. The cops will be here soon, and we don't want to spend the rest of the day talking to them downtown."

"You're right," Lars said. Then his face brightened. "Instead, why don't we go see what they're up to in that country warehouse?"

CHAPTER 25

THEY LEFT THE house and quickly advanced up the alleyway out onto the street. Sam led them over to the black SUV. He got in the driver's seat. "Okay, lead us to this warehouse that you were telling us about, Lars."

"Fine. My motorcycle is parked around the corner. I suggest that you both follow me out there."

They drove down the street and stopped at Lars's motorcycle. He got on, turned the ignition, gave Sam and Fredric a thumbs-up sign, and pulled out. They headed down South Street, looking around for any signs of activity. Sure enough, a police siren started whooping behind them. Yet it was off in the distance, and it was headed to a destination they were leaving behind.

"That Lars is pretty cold-blooded," Sam remarked to Fredric, "daring that guy to shoot."

Fredric gave Sam an assessing look. He couldn't be sure, but he guessed that Sam had never fired his service revolver before outside of training. He seemed pretty shaken up. As they continued to drive, Fredric's thoughts turned to how the shooting went down. He frowned as he replied, "He's probably right, that the guy wouldn't have talked. Still, I wanted the chance to find out." He looked out the windshield as the motorcycle veered at the corner and took a right. "Not bad with his gun, though. We may need that, where we're going."

After twenty minutes of driving, Lars took an exit ramp off the interstate. The SUV quickly followed. "We must be getting close," Fredric told Sam. The two had said little other than listen to rock on WMMR. Not a bad station, Fredric thought.

A truck stop was near the off-ramp. Lars pulled in and parked his motorcycle on the outer perimeter. He got into the back seat of the SUV. "Okay, let's drive by the building that the guy I followed earlier went to. But we better not stop or go inside until we are sure what we are doing. We don't want to tip them off." Lars pointed his hand in between the two front seats. "Pull back out of the parking lot, and turn right."

After no more than a few minutes of driving, Lars spoke up. "Coming up there. On the right. That was the building."

Sam drove slowly by the warehouse. Lars noted that there were three cars parked outside.

"We would be foolish to just pull up in front," Fredric noted.

"Better to approach on foot and surprise them," Lars suggested.

Sam contributed his own thought. "As high tech as these people are, they probably have sophisticated motion detectors or other perimeter monitoring equipment. So we would have no better success than just driving up in a black SUV with tinted windows. Plus, we have no idea what we will find inside. You just don't go walking into a big windowless building that you think is being used for criminal activity without being prepared for the worst-case scenario of being outmanned and outgunned. It is time for me to call in my colleagues. We'll conduct a massive raid."

Not in a million years, Fredric thought to himself. "Let's talk about it first."

They pulled up a short distance down the road.

"How do you know no one in your office hasn't been compromised?" Fredric asked.

After a short back and forth, Fredric got out his phone and pulled a scrap of paper from his pocket. He then punched some numbers into the phone. Sam and Lars looked at him as he placed the phone up to his ear.

"Jason here." The attorney general was on the line.

Fredric summed up what had transpired and what needed to be done next.

There was a long silence on the phone.

"Hold on, I have met someone along the way who is on our team as well. I don't really understand who he is, but he's already been a big asset to us."

Fredric handed the phone to Lars.

"Look, mister," he said firmly. "There is a CEO of a bank involved. You might know his name and his bank if I said it. More likely, you wouldn't, but your team in Los Angeles does. I have a videotaped confession from him. To be specific, he admits that he was helping Srepska launder money and use the financial system for illegal purposes. He gave me the information that led me to this location. I can tell you where the head of that bank is right now and how to get the evidence. There is a clear nexus between him, Srepska, the bank, and the building we need to storm."

Lim didn't answer right away. "Oh god, you can't be serious. Wait, is Sam there? Let me talk to Sam," Lim interrupted.

Sam answered Lim's questions to confirm that Lars seemed legitimate. He described the house in downtown Philadelphia and how Lars and Fredric ended up there independently. Sam told Lim that it was worth taking a chance on what Lars had to say.

Several long moments elapsed as Fredric and Lars wondered what the two men were planning, as Lim was doing most of the talking.

"Okay, talk soon," Sam said. "We have a plan. It is on a fast track."

About three minutes later, Sam's phone rang.

On the other line were Lim, the Chief of the Justice Department's National Security Branch, and a senior U.S. Attorney in

Los Angeles assigned to national security cases. "Are we ready?" the Chief asked. Sam answered yes.

"I swear to tell the truth and nothing but the truth. I am Sam Davis, a federal law enforcement officer with the FBI's Washington Field Office. I request a search warrant and state under penalty of perjury that I have reason to believe that at 222 Bethel Road in Aston, Pennsylvania, within the Eastern Judicial District of Pennsylvania, there is a warehouse that contains certain computers, computer equipment, computer files, phones, drives used for computer data storage, and other relevant documents, files and records that are evidence relevant to an act of computer hacking. Specifically, several sections of Title 18 U.S. Code Section 1030 states that anyone who accesses a computer without authorization is guilty of a crime, as is anyone who transmits a program or command via a computer to intentionally cause damage. The facts that I have just recited are based on information from an informant that he followed a white male subject into this address about three hours ago today from a known crime scene in nearby Philadelphia. The informant said that the person who fled the crime scene was driving a gray Ford sedan, and I personally observed while driving on the public street in front of the building that there was a gray Ford sedan in the parking lot."

Sam continued to talk for a couple more minutes as he further described the location he planned to search and more details about what he hoped to find.

"Further, I have reason to believe that the computer crimes are being used to perpetrate an act of domestic terrorism in violation of Section 2331 of Title 18 of the U.S. Code."

Lars and Fredric looked at each other. Fredric raised his eyebrows, and Lars cracked a smile.

"So, Your Honor, I request this warrant to enter and search the premises. I further request a 'no knock' warrant so we can enter the building immediately upon arrival, given that I believe the people inside are heavily armed. Specifically, I have information to suggest that they have ties with a violent crime ring in Europe. And, we believe they can conduct sophisticated monitoring of communications, so after we execute the warrant, we will request approval to keep the warrant under seal to avoid tipping our hand to them."

There was a long pause. "Thank you, Your Honor. Yes, I will."

Sam pulled the phone away from his ear and pushed the button to end the call.

"We got the warrant," Sam told Fredric and Lars. "The judge is going to fax the warrant to the Philadelphia Field Office. The Justice Department National Security Section Chief is calling the Philadelphia Field Office and is directing them not to enter the case into any computer. And only the head of the office will know what is going on. All the agents who are helping execute the search are going to think they are investigating a run of the mill gang case. So, assuming Srepska doesn't have an undercover operative in the Philadelphia office, it's a pretty airtight way to do this without tipping Srepska off. A rapid response team will meet us here in about sixty minutes."

Both Fredric and Lars looked unhappy at this turn of events. They were being boxed out of an operation that they had done so much to set in motion.

Sam sensed the problem, and he told Fredric, "Look in the glove compartment. They should be right there."

Fredric did as he asked, and on top of a pile of laminated cards were several badges reading "FBI."

"Congratulations," Sam said. "You two have been unofficially deputized."

Lars looked like he wanted no part of it, but Fredric pulled them out. Each was attached to a lanyard, and he hung one around his neck. "From the BND to the FBI. If I keep this up, pretty soon I'll have a collection."

He turned to hand one to Lars, and when he remained sitting stiffly, Fredric reached back and hung it himself. "There," he said with a satisfied smile. "Now we're still all together."

CHAPTER 26

SUVS HAD BEEN arriving from several directions. The windows in all of them were blacked out, hiding any activities of the passengers inside. Fredric could guess that they were putting on assault gear. He wanted to do the same.

"Okay, the team is going to be here any minute now," Sam announced. "We are going to need to split up once we rush inside. I will accompany the rest of the FBI team to serve the search warrant on the warehouse. You will have to hang back." He spoke to both of them, but he was looking straight at Lars as he added, "You can't do any shooting unless it's life or death. It will be a big hassle if any civilians kill someone. I could get fired. Do you understand me?"

"I don't have to kill anyone else today," Fredric said.

"Yeah, we'll hang back," Lars added, though he didn't look like he liked the idea one bit.

"As long as we're clear on that," Sam said. "Any damage would never fly with the guys helping me."

"As long as we get inside," Lars said. "I didn't fly all the way out from California to shoot the breeze."

"Fine. Now, listen. I'm going to tell them that you two are IT guys. They know that this is a hacker bust. Okay? You both have your covers. You are working with me. I will tell the lead agent, and you guys come in right after the advance team breaks through. Follow what I do and try to fit in."

They stepped out of the vehicle and stretched their legs after the long drive. They soon saw a helicopter make a loop around the area before flying off. Four unmarked SUVs pulled up in a line down the road, and Sam flashed a thumbs-up to each of them. Someone got out of the front passenger seat of each of the SUVs. "They are here," Sam said as they walked over. "Let's go."

Unlike Sam, all the men had helmets, knee protectors, elbow pads, heavy bullet-resistant armor, and were dressed in matching dark green uniforms. Each was carrying a sub-machine gun, and Fredric noticed the sidearms holstered on their waists. Sam went over to one of them and they started talking quietly. Sam gestured several times at Fredric and Lars, apparently to explain why they were there.

"Here, suit up with this stuff."

One of the agents handed several pieces of equipment to Sam. Sam stepped aside and put on the items.

Soon, Sam was wearing a bulletproof vest and a jacket that displayed FBI on the back, with his FBI badge hanging around his neck. "Follow me," Sam told the assembled assault squad.

They filed down the road cautiously, weapons parked at their sides. Sam and Fredric had already scoped out the warehouse while they were waiting, and they had spotted no signs of any type of surveillance camera. In pairs, they entered the near end of the parking lot. Quietly, hugging the front wall, most of them advanced to the door. Three agents were assigned to stand outside the loading dock, and two other agents were posted alongside a side door. That way everyone would stay trapped inside.

"Okay," Sam said in a hush, "let's bring up the ram." The team of agents congregated around both sides of the door as two other agents brought out a battering ram. "We're going in, on the count of three."

Back and forth swung the ram, gathering momentum so that the first strike against the door would bust it wide open.

"One, two, three!"

The two men swung the ram violently forward, and the door gave way with an explosion of splinters.

"Let's go!"

The first team rushed forward, weapons drawn. Fredric wanted to be the first to run inside the building, as he had done so many times before. But he waited until the squad had raced past him.

Inside, he could hear the shouts: "Put your hands up on your heads! All of you! Put those hands up where we can see them!"

Fredric and Lars rushed inside themselves. They had entered a long, darkened cavern filled with empty shelving along one long wall. A few spotlights lit the back. Two very large vehicles stood near the oversized garage doors, and Fredric strained in the gloom to see what they were.

Beyond the line of FBI agents, all with their guns at the ready, were several tables around which a group of men and women were assembled. As the line of agents advanced, Fredric could see all the laptops on the tables. Beyond were racks and racks of servers. If this wasn't the mother lode, they had hit some vital artery.

"Get your hands up, ass-wipe!"

The agents stormed forward, and several holstered their rifles in order to start putting handcuffs on the captured tech crew. As the line of uniforms parted, Fredric could see that they were dressed casually, like computer techs anywhere. They hardly looked like criminals who were bent on destroying the financial networks of the United States.

All of a sudden one of them burst into a run, trying to flee to the back of the warehouse. He hadn't taken ten steps before Sam's rifle fired with a loud retort. With an agonized cry the man flung out his arms and crashed face first to the floor. He writhed in a heap as several FBI agents rushed over to him.

"Does anyone else have any bright ideas?" Sam shouted.

Soon all the rest of the Srepska crew had their hands pinioned in handcuffs. About half of the agents started to escort them out of the building. Another small group sat down in front of one computer apiece. *These must be the FBI's real techies,* Fredric guessed.

With the Srepska crew mopped up, Fredric and Lars took a long look around the warehouse.

"This used to be an auto repair facility," Lars pointed out. "Why else would there be those big bays? And look at the oil and grease stains all over the concrete."

Both of them blinked when simultaneously, all the lights in the warehouse turned on. Blinded at first, Fredric soon recovered and his attention was drawn to shadowy vehicles he had seen upon coming inside. There were three red firetrucks that had Washington, DC Fire Department signs and stickers.

"Hey," Lars said, "what are firetrucks from DC doing here?"

Suddenly, Fredric looked up. The bright lights had revealed a small, isolated room, built in one corner of the large open space that was the second floor. *I bet the room was used to keep watch on employees who used to work here,* he thought.

One tall and heavily muscled agent filed up a circular metal staircase, followed single file by two men. At the top of the stairs was a door leading into the room.

The crack of a single shot echoed through the warehouse. The duo froze as they spotted a figure standing in the window. With his rifle he was breaking the glass open.

Fredric grasped his intention right away. He meant to fire down at the agent coming up the stairwell before they could arrest him. Without hesitation, he pulled his firearm and locked his arms. He fired a single shot that blasted the silence of the large space. A red hole appeared in the man's forehead and he was flung backward. The wall behind him was splattered with gore.

Almost simultaneously a half dozen shots rang out. The man's body twitched with all of the bullets and he dropped out of sight below the window.

By that time, Fredric had already holstered his weapon. He

couldn't be sure if anyone saw what he did, but he wasn't going to tell unless someone approached him.

Lars cracked a slight smile as a neutral expression filled Fredric's face. "I saw what you did, partner," he whispered. "That was a helluva shot. You probably saved those guys' bacon."

Off to their side, a man emerged from behind the server racks. Seeing him, Sam and several other agents raised their rifles. "On the ground, now!" came Sam's firm voice.

The footsteps of the agents became louder as they walked toward the man. "Drop the gun. On the ground now!" Sam shouted in an almost frantic voice. The man froze.

The man began to bend down as if to put his gun down. But he quickly pulled the barrel of his gun up toward the agents.

The man's chest was thrown back by a triple blast of gunshots that was quickly followed by a fusillade of fire.

Lars and Fredric looked at each other. "I wonder if there are any more rats that are going to come out of the woodwork," Lars said.

"Probably not," Fredric replied. "In any case, come with me. We have to take a closer look at those firetrucks."

CHAPTER 27

"ALL EIGHT OF these perps can be arrested for firearms viola-
tions. There are four Eastern European sub-machine guns without
serial numbers over here," one agent shouted to another.

In the meantime, Fredric and Lars walked a full circuit around
the trucks. They started opening the doors and compartments on
the sides of the first truck to look for anything that might be amiss
or other contraband. They were quickly joined by a half dozen FBI
agents. A U.S. flag was still hanging on a pole on the back of one
of the fire engines. Seeing the FBI agents at work, Fredric decided
to climb under the fire engines and look for any clues.

He got down on his knees and slid under the first fire truck.
Those large mufflers must get hot when the truck operates, he thought.
I hope I can fit under the axle assembly. He crawled under on his
back and noticed something strange. *Why don't I feel cold concrete
under me? It feels like a stiff carpet of some sort.* He felt around and
turned his head sideways. He didn't have enough space to roll over.

Fredric climbed back out from under and called for Sam, who
now was making an inventory with the other agents of what they
had discovered.

"You see the big rugs under each of these trucks. I guess they
are supposed to catch any fuel or other leakages from the trucks.
Well, there is something under the rug that is under that truck,
and I think we need to move the truck to find out. Look carefully

at the blanket. See that small sag in the center, as if it is draped over a hole? Notice how that isn't the case with the other rugs," he said while pointing to the other fire engines.

"Hey guys, anyone seen the keys to these fire engines?" Sam shouted to his colleagues.

"Yeah man, I saw a bunch of keys on the table over there," a younger agent noted. He walked toward a table on the far side of the firetrucks.

He got them and tossed them to Sam. Sam tossed them to Fredric. Several of the team of agents walked over to watch.

Fredric climbed up into the cab of the truck. Lars climbed up on the other side, and the two men quietly conferred out of earshot.

"It's just like my days in the military," Fredric informed him. "I drove big rigs like this all the time. Never drove a firetruck."

"There's always a first time," Lars said with a laugh.

Sam raised his hand for a high five, and after a moment of hesitation Fredric slapped with him.

"Let's see, which one is the key that unlocks the door?" The third key on the ring that Fredric tried worked, and the engine on the truck purred.

He drove the truck forward far enough to completely expose the place underneath where the truck had been parked.

Two of the agents grabbed one side of the carpet. With a heave, they pulled it toward them.

"There's a door there," one of the agents remarked. Suddenly, a square concrete ring posted on a wooden door set into the floor was visible.

"Who has a screwdriver?" Sam shouted.

"Here let's try this," another agent replied as he bent down with what appeared to be a heavy-duty pocketknife. Yet the door didn't budge an inch.

"That won't work," Sam said. "Thing is probably locked from below."

Soon an agent walked over with a crowbar. *That is probably not going to work either,* Lars thought as he saw how little space there was between the door and doorframe.

"I bet there is a wine cellar down there," one young agent said sarcastically. No one responded. They were still trying to jam the working end of the crowbar to open the door.

Fredric walked back to the firetruck. He opened several doors until he found what he had spied a few minutes earlier. "Try this," he said, walking over with an axe.

After several ferocious swings, an agent smashed the door open. "Why didn't we see the small bolt on the side in the frame? That was what was keeping it shut," he said.

"FBI agents. Is anyone down there?" Sam yelled as he got on his knees and shined his flashlight down.

"Help us, please. Our hands and ankles are bound and we cannot move," they heard a middle-age man say with an authoritative voice.

Sam shined his flashlight around until he found four people standing in the square hole. Sure enough, they were all bound with ropes. "I guess we can add kidnapping to the charges," he muttered to Fredric.

There didn't appear to be a ladder or other way to get down, though. The floor looked about twelve feet down.

One of the agents put his gun aside. "I'll go in and see what's down there." He climbed in, grabbing the edge of the floor, and dropped down with a loud thump as he landed.

Within moments, he found a light switch to illuminate the area below. Everyone on top was by now looking down. Four men in suits had their wrists and hands bound.

The agent who went down suddenly yelled out in shock.

Sam cried down to him, "Are they hostages?"

The agent yelled, "You won't believe who is down here. Get some ropes and haul these guys out of here."

More doors were opened on the trucks until a sturdy rope was found. In the meantime, the agent had cut each of the trussed-up men loose. With the rope end dangling around his head, he pulled it down and wound it around the chest of one of the hostages.

"Okay, haul him up!"

Four agents manned the rope and pulled up the dead weight. As the man's head emerged above the floor, everyone in the room gasped with shock.

"Is that you, Mr. President," Sam asked.

"Yes. Thank the lord you showed up. I was wondering how long we were going to be down there. Where is the Vice President?"

"Not so fast," Sam said. "How long have you been down there?"

"It's been several days. I was knocked out in the Treasury building, and when I woke up, I was in that foul hole."

Sam was seriously confused. "You look like the president I have seen on TV, but I just heard you give a press conference on the radio. How did you get there? When?"

"Hold on," another agent said. "I don't know if this is the President, but these men clearly were being held against their will. Their safety and well-being is our concern now.".

"These men with me are my Secret Service agents," the President said. "I don't remember much of what happened. I just remember falling to the ground, and then when I woke up, cloth was tied around my eyes and my hands were bound. They must have drugged me. But I'm worried stiff about the country. We're in the middle of a terrible crisis. I need to talk to the Vice President now along with my national security team."

Fredric and Lars were staring at the man open-mouthed. Yet even amid his shock, the tumblers were turning in Lars's mind. Everyone had said how strange it was that the President had ordered the U.S. to invade Myanmar. And here was a man claiming to be the real President. The real President would have never given such an order.

Fredric elbowed Lars slightly in the ribs. "Do you see what I'm seeing?"

He pointed toward the top corner of the warehouse closest to them. Hidden almost completely in the shadows was a small glass eye. "A video camera."

"That means…"

Fredric supplied the rest: "Srepska is watching our every move. Including whoever is sitting in the White House rather than the man we just found."

"Right. Rather than the President."

The stakes of the Srepska gamble had suddenly become much bigger.

CHAPTER 28

WHILE ALL THIS was happening, Sam walked over to Fredric and Lars. "Hey…"

"We need to talk," Fredric said in an agitated voice. "Very important."

"Yes. Let's go into that room over there," Sam said, pointing to a small office nearby. As they entered the room, they saw it had a table and some chairs, along with a sink and an office refrigerator. It appeared to have been used as a break room.

As soon as they were out of earshot of the others, Fredric vented his agitation at how Sam and the FBI were handling the situation.

"Right now, every Srepska asset across the country knows about what just happened. How? Your agents are standing in front of webcams in every corner of the building. The guys we are after probably watched everything that happened."

Sam responded, "I see where you are going. The man in the White House—if he is an imposter—can issue orders to contain us and keep it all this under wraps."

"We need to move fast," Lars jumped in. "We have to conduct a similar raid on the White House as we did here now, take everyone aside and interview them. As their legitimacy status, if you will, is being confirmed, the President returns to his office. The public wouldn't even have to know what happened."

Sam walked outside and pulled aside the lead agent from the Philadelphia field office.

Lars and Fredric listened to the back and forth between the man claiming to be President and the confused agents trying to determine how to proceed. Shortly, Sam walked up to the President and handed him a phone. "Here. Make a call."

The President called his Chief of Staff and explained what had happened.

"I thought something was amiss," Campbell remarked. "There was something about the *you* I saw that just didn't seem right. But my instinct tells me that you should stay on the outside for a few hours. I can delay any decisions the imposter wants to make. If we don't do this right, you and the people who rescued you could get cast off as crackpots. The man downstairs may accuse me of trying to stage a coup and have us arrested or who knows what. We don't know who else they have working for them. Is it just the people down in the bunker or are there others? They had to have help. This is tricky."

"That's nonsense. I talk to the press, everyone will know it is me," the President said.

"First, you have to get reporters to even talk to you. You know how they are solicited by crackpots all the time. Then, even once they know it is you, how are they going to reconcile it with the other president in the White House who says the nation is under attack? Yes, everyone will soon believe you, but I am just saying we need to take it slow and do this carefully so we don't get squelched before you can get to safety."

"I still don't like this idea."

Campbell continued. "Plus, we don't know what else they have up their sleeve. We bring you out too quickly and who knows what they may have planned and will unleash. Just let me consult with law enforcement and figure a good path."

"I see your point. I want what is best for the country. Assess the scope of the problem and contain the terrorists."

Campbell then called Lim and told him what had happened.

"That's a relief, knowing that. What happened during the cabinet meeting was unusual," Lim said. "He had never called me by my last name like he did at the meeting, and he sounded ruder and curter than the President Evans I know."

"Yes, I knew something was wrong," Campbell replied. "He didn't want me or his personal assistant, the first lady, or anyone else to go down with him."

"My instincts tell me that we lure the man in the bunker along with the men with him. We get them to go somewhere off the White House premises and then game over. Let me consult with the Secret Service and get people on the phone who have experience with this," Lim continued.

"I have got to take this call," Sam said about ten minutes later as he stepped away from a huddle with his fellow agents. Several short moments later, Sam hung up the phone and shouted to all. "I just got confirmation of what we all wanted to believe. President Evans is here in our midst. There is a man in the Oval Office who is an imposter. He is going to get coaxed out of the White House along with his co-conspirator entourage. Until we can contain the security breach, we need to get Mr. President to a safe place that is NOT—repeat NOT—here. Lim will get us space at the dorms connected to the FBI's training facility on a military base in Northern Virginia. We need to move NOW," he said with urgency.

One of the agents who had been standing around surfing the web on his phone shouted out in a loud voice. "Hey guys, you have to see this."

"Check this out. There is breaking news. Throughout Chicago, traffic lights have suddenly stopped working. Lights just went off in businesses without backup power supplies, and central heating systems stopped blowing. The power system had a major failure and it's impacting the entire Chicago area. And there is no worse time for the power and heat to go off in Chicago than the middle of winter."

Sam was reading his phone as well. "Well, compounding the problem, the power grid problems that originated in Chicago are quickly starting to expand and leave increasingly large swaths of the Midwest without power according to CNBC."

Within a few moments, the lights started to flicker in the warehouse. Then the lights went off. The background whirling sound of the central ventilation system suddenly went quiet. Off in a distance, the Exit signs suddenly were illuminated as their batteries kicked in.

All the agents drew their guns. Several crouched and aimed the guns at the doors. The group of agents broke into two groups toward each of the doors in sight. Two agents advanced toward each door. One agent quickly opened the door. They then went outside each door. Within several moments, the word "Clear" was shouted outside of each door.

The warehouse wasn't under attack, you fools, Lars thought. "The power grid is automated and susceptible to internet attacks," Fredric quickly piped up as agents reached for their blackberries or other smartphones. "So much for a safe and resilient power system as the energy companies claim," Lars added.

"This is distinctly the work of Srepska," Fredric said authoritatively under his breath to Lars.

"How could these people bring down the power system?" a young agent asked.

There was silence until Lars spoke up. "Easy. You would target the supervisory control modules for one or more power grids. If you do it strategically, you can wreak havoc with power grids across the nation by targeting just a few places since they are all interconnected. You could cause a cascading failure by having something critical fail, because then other elements of the system are going to automatically pick up the slack. Those other parts will overload. And, power surges will reverberate throughout the system and cook some transformers, not to mention sensitive electronics of consumers, so suddenly you are adding a digit to the number of days that it will take to recover. You could cause temporary damage, or you could send signals to cause machines and transmission equipment to self-destruct…"

"Self-destruct?" the young agent furrowed his brow and looked at Lars.

Sam piped up with the answer. "Yes, it is called cyber warfare. It's been used to target the nuclear plans of rogue states, just search the web and you can learn more. That's not our problem to fix or worry about now," Sam said.

Lars began thinking. *It can be nearly impossible to track down who originates these attacks. But the way I found out the lead that got me here was searching internet traffic logs and money flows. Sure, every lead takes you on a very circuitous path. But I know what I am doing and can figure it out."*

Fredric wondered what other developments the criminal organization may be plotting that were not captured during his brief surveillance in Budapest. *Could the next episode be more sinister or deadly?*

Sitting around a large table miles away, several men and a woman were staring – motionless—at the images of Lars and Fredric from the warehouse. The only sound was the hum of the power generators outdoors.

"The FBI we can identify, with their jackets and all. But have we figured out yet who these two jokers are and how they found us?" Natasha asked.

All of them were looking at a video monitor on which Zoltan could be seen. He was pacing to and fro through his working area back in Budapest.

"That German operative is the same guy who knocked off two

of our men in Városliget city park here. He is talking to that tall blond guy and those two seem to be standing by themselves. Is the blond guy another German operative?"

"He must be the same guy who took out Kruno back at the house in Philadelphia where we were routing all the internet traffic. He can't be police."

"Have we figured out who he is yet," said Zoltan as he smoked furiously on a cigar.

"I guess he is a German intelligence agent too. He must be the internet sleuth of the duo."

"No," Zoltan said. "How is it progressing with the facial recognition of him? Stop thinking small. Tap our entire networks, our resources, figure this out."

"I just realized that there was another camera outside that was able to get us a good glimpse at the license plate of the motorcycle this guy rode up on. How are we going to be sure that we will really be able to run the plate through now that both of our Pennsylvania facilities have been found?" Natasha asked.

"It's a good thing that we did contingency planning for this," Zoltan growled. "Messing with the power grid will buy us more time and disrupt any plans they might have."

An operative back in Budapest approached Zoltan and showed him an email on his phone. "They got to our bank contact too, the one out in L.A." His voice gained more urgency. "We need to find who penetrated us."

Meanwhile, one of his operatives had contacted the Hungarian Security Services to use a facial-recognition program to try to identify who the tall blond guy was. He shouted out to Zoltan. "Blondie is an assassin for hire. He lives in Pasadena, California. No tie to Germany at all from what we can tell."

"Why would someone like that be coming after us like this? He's not an investigator, yet that's what it seems like here."

At the same time, Natasha received some news on her laptop.

"The license plate you asked me to check on is registered to a mail drop—a packaging store that rents out mailboxes for people to receive mail– in Long Beach, California. The name the car is registered under is George T. Lostowitz. The phrase *get lost* is fairly obvious to me...it is clearly a fake name. Do you think that this same guy took our banker?" she asked.

Zoltan shouted, now sounding more confident, "Natasha, new job. Find and kill these people. Send a message to who they are working for. These two came after us, and now I am after them. We have no excuses now that we have their pictures."

CHAPTER 29

IN THE WAREHOUSE, the lead agent proceeded to split his team into three. One team led by Sam would drive the President and Secret Service agents, one team would conduct the initial interrogation and then transport the prisoners to Philadelphia, and the third would secure the outside of the facility until the evidence-collection team specialists arrived to comb the building and catalogue all the evidence.

Meanwhile, Lars was snapping a picture of a map tacked up to a bulletin board behind the table. It had a thumbtack around a circle of a map—a map that he noticed was of downtown Washington, DC. He then placed his hand on the table as if to lean on it. He grabbed a ring of keys attached to an ID card. He immediately recognized a chip on it and knew it was a government ID card. Swiftly, he placed it in his pocket. He looked around and felt smug knowing that no one had seen what he did.

Fredric felt his phone ring. It was his boss.

"Fredric, I heard what happened at the warehouse. Good work. I am proud of you. Are you taking care of yourself?"

Fredric paused. "For the moment. But maybe not for long the way the FBI is bumbling this investigation. There are cameras everywhere, but no one seemed to notice or care that they might be connected somewhere. The safety of everyone here is at risk. Where's the mole? What happened to her?"

"Nobody knows."

"Vanished? Just gone without a trace? When did that happen? Who are her friends at work who might know ways to find her?" Fredric asked.

"She only just came in with the new administration."

"You don't know? Well, who does know? How can you find out?"

"I suggest you pay Lim another visit. He might have information that you need. Can you get back to Washington?"

"Of course, I can. They are sending a detail of the FBI down there as we speak."

They chatted another minute, then concluded the call.

Conflicting thoughts crossed Fredric's mind. *Am I being played for a fool by the FBI? But if that were the case, how would we have ended up taking down two Srepska outposts on his watch, one clearly a server farm for their operations and another where they were holding the President of the United States hostage as a double starts World War III. Plus, Sam and his FBI crew seem trustworthy.*

Of them all, the Californian operative was the one he trusted the most at this moment. He went over and said in a low voice, "Lars, I have decided to go meet up with Jason Lim again. He could have inside information on a Srepska operative I need to track down. You can come with me if you want. If you do—"

"No. No way. I need the freedom to pursue leads of my own," Lars said. "But hey, I will drop you off in Washington. I am going down there anyway. I think Pennsylvania has been tapped out."

Meanwhile, Fredric thought to himself how being with Sam and the rest of the gang could be a liability if his theory about the cameras were right…and if the people they were after had deeper connections than anyone realized.

Fredric nodded to Lars. To the FBI agent he said, "It's been great working with you Sam. I see you got your hands full right here, so I am going to leave now. Let's talk soon. You should have everything you need to wrap this up from here, you got the President, you got criminals captured, you got laptops and computers that your forensics people can scrub for evidence. And you should be able to use it to track down the current problem with the financial system, and it looks like now the power grid. You don't need me anymore, right?" Fredric said.

They soon agreed to go their separate ways.

Sam added, "We will talk again, but it's best, if asked, we all deny ever having worked together. My internal affairs unit would have a field day if they ever found out that I worked with either of you extra-judicially. So, get going. Here I will walk you out."

They went outside, which seemed extremely bright after the dimness in the warehouse. Lars got on the motorcycle, put on his helmet, and Fredric jumped on the passenger's seat. Lars floored the motorcycle and they zoomed off toward the highway.

On the way to the interstate, they passed a late-model gray Toyota Corolla. Inside, Fredric noticed as they passed, were two younger men, one wearing a leather jacket and the other wearing a jacket with a bear on the chest. The driver stared at them, and Fredric had the distinct impression he was Slavic.

As they drove onto the highway ramp, another detail he had seen kicked in with him. There had been a bar code in the back window, which meant it was a rental car. Fredric looked in his side-view mirror. "A rental car with Virginia plates on a backwood road in Pennsylvania."

What he didn't know was that behind them on Interstate 95 would soon be a convoy of three SUVs.

CHAPTER 30

LARS DROVE THE motorcycle, with Fredric on the back, to downtown DC on Connecticut Avenue. The Beltway was a parking lot, with so many cars apparently leaving the city. Most of the traffic lights were out. They noticed that lights were off in most businesses. Only those that had backup generators had lights. It was starting to get dusk. At several key intersections police officers were directing traffic. Traffic was moving very slowly, but Lars expertly navigated his motorcycle around the cars to maintain a steady speed.

Lars stopped his motorbike just south of DuPont Circle. "I think this is about a quarter mile from Farragut Square. Let's split up here," he said.

Fredric responded, "It has been delightful working with you. I have a feeling our paths will cross again, or at least I hope they do."

"If we don't talk by phone, let's touch base by posting a message for a used red 1974 Volkswagen Ghia on Craigslist. We will both monitor it and whoever sees it will contact the other. We will ask the seller if the car could do a trip to Philadelphia. That will be the keyword, all right?" Lars said.

"Sounds doable, but what is Craigslist," Fredric asked.

"It's a popular online classified board here in the United States. It's simple and easy to use…you don't need a credit card or anything to pay for an ad," Lars said.

"Sounds like a plan," Fredric said.

Fredric walked until he noticed he was at Farragut Square again. Conflicting thoughts passed through his mind. Should he call his boss in Germany for further directions? What if he were walking into a trap? He took the phone out of his backpack and turned it on. The battery icon was red. "Cheap useless prepaid phones," he muttered under his breath. He dialed a number.

A groggy voice was on the other side of the line. "Am I alone? Are there others working on this case?" he asked, using an encrypted code that only he and his boss Walter Schneider had.

There was silence. Walter replied in code, "What are you talking about?"

"I met someone. Someone from Los Angeles who told me he took this case because of the money. I want to know, is he real or is he fake?"

Walter paused again. "Our analyst team thinks there was a West Coast tie to Srepska. We captured some information besides what you had found. It was actionable. Yes, you are not alone. But anyone else is simply an asset to what you are trying to accomplish. It has no reflection on our confidence in you," Walter replied in code.

"Fine," Fredric said. "We are going to solve this soon," he added. "I will see you before long."

Fredric put the phone back in his backpack and continued walking. *How many Lars are there?* he wondered. Soon he approached Farragut Square. Just as before, he noticed a black SUV waiting. There was a female agent inside this time. She flashed the red and blue lights in the car as he waited to cross the street to approach the park.

The SUV started to pull forward. It was clear the driver knew who he was.

The passenger-side window was rolled down. He noticed that the driver was wearing well-fitting blue jeans and a t-shirt that said,

"Gavels Softball Team." She was about thirty years old. He saw a walkie-talkie along with an emergency light on the dashboard. Only it was red, unlike the blue light Sam had. There was a white piece of paper on the dashboard. He imagined that it probably said, "Official Police Vehicle" with the FBI logo on the other side, just as the sign in Sam's SUV.

"Jason Lim sent me. You are Fredric, right?"

"Yes, good to meet you. Looks like you are undercover just like I am," he said.

"Yeah, no one would ever guess," she said with a chuckle. "But if we want people to know we are legitimate, we just put on jackets and badges. I have a set for both of us in the back if we ever need them. Hop in," she said as the door electronically unlocked.

"I am Natasha," she said as she stretched out her arm to Fredric. He noticed that her hands were well manicured. "It looks like you could use a good shower and a change of clothes. I smell exhaust on you," she said calmly.

"Yes, I just got off a motorcycle. But the clock is ticking and will not wait for me. Let's go to see Attorney General Lim."

"He actually told me to take you to a facility outside the Beltway, where the President and his men are being taken to by your buddy, Sam Davis. He briefed the real President about your role in finding them, and now the President wants you to go there and talk to him."

Why would the President of the United States want to have me in his company? Then Fredric thought back to Sam. *Did the President see me and then ask Sam who I was? Or maybe Lim passed the word along,* Fredric thought. "Fine. I am glad Lim changed his mind. By the way, do I hear a hint of a Croatian accent in your voice?"

"Yes, I grew up in a Croatian family in Chicago," she said as she drove out of Farragut Square with the lights activated, enabling them to get through traffic more quickly. "You know, we will be going right by my apartment. How about we stop quickly so you can shower and get that fuel smell off you?"

"I don't want to keep the president or attorney general waiting. I have a job to do, and they are my key to do it," he said. "Let's get to the destination and then we can worry about that."

"The attorney general won't be there for another hour. I just talked to him before you arrived. We have time to make a quick stop."

This is odd, he thought. *Even if Lim won't be arriving until later.* On the other hand, though, he was looking for Srepska. If this woman had her own agenda, she might be the lead he needed. His hand tightened slightly on his pistol as he agreed. "That would be nice. I do feel grubby."

They drove up Connecticut Avenue north of downtown about two miles and crossed a bridge. They then stopped at a five-story apartment building in the middle of a block of other older but well-maintained apartments on a leafy, tree-lined street. She drove into the circular driveway and parked. "No one is going to tow this car with the FBI sign in the front," she chuckled.

"I imagine that writing parking tickets is the last priority right now for the police department given how traffic is and everything else going on," Fredric replied.

They walked by the two elevators that had their doors open. The lights were on in the elevators, but dimmer than would normally be expected. "Looks like they are out of service because of the power problems. I am on the fourth floor. Guess we need to use the stairs," she said.

"Okay. You lead the way."

They opened the staircase, which was dimly lit. She went up the stairs, and his thoughts alternated between watching her well-shaped derriere and staying alert for any strange moves she made.

On the fourth floor, they entered the hallway and she led the way to her apartment. She opened the door, and they both walked in.

"My next-door neighbor is about your size. I bet I could

borrow a set of nice clothes for you from him if he is home," she said.

Fredric looked around. It was a studio apartment that looked barely lived in. There was a queen-sized bed in the corner, with a long couch, and several guest chairs facing a flat-screen TV. A laptop was perched on the couch. The large window looked out on a courtyard, which was surrounded by other apartments in the building. With its lack of a woman's personal touches, it looked distinctly like a short-stay apartment.

"The bathroom is down there," she said as she pointed toward the walk-in closet, behind which Fredric saw a small but newish-looking bathroom. "Can I get you something to drink or maybe snack on?"

"It's really important that we get to our destination as quickly as possible. We don't have time to relax. But what do you have? Maybe we have time for a small early dinner. I have a feeling it will be a long night."

"I could sure use a glass of wine right now. Maybe you could use a drink? I can heat up some burgers. Luckily, my oven is gas, so we can still use it even though the power is out."

"Fabulous. And, oh I don't need a change of clothes, I have one in my backpack. But thanks for the offer."

He walked into the shower. He took off his clothes carefully, listening for any sounds of her approaching. He still couldn't be sure she was being anything but friendly. He'd heard Americans were like that. Still, he lifted his Walther P4 out of its shoulder holster and laid it on the sink rim, conveniently right next to the shower stall. And he twisted his body to face the door the entire time he was showering.

Yet Natasha never showed, and that told him something important. She needed him alive—so he could get her within range of the President.

CHAPTER 31

GERGELY WAS EXHAUSTED from sitting in the downstairs situation room for so long. Zoltan hadn't told him what he should do otherwise. He could hardly go up to the Oval Office, because someone would recognize that he wasn't the real thing. Yet staying down here was making him look increasingly odd. A president had other duties besides declaring an attack on a foreign country.

"Is it me," he said softly in Hungarian to his "bodyguard," "or is it getting very hot suddenly?"

"No, I've noticed it too. Someone must have turned up the heat. I'm starting to bake."

"I wish Zoltan would tell us we're free to go."

What Gergely didn't say was the pressing point that he'd been thinking more and more as the hours wended past. Maybe Zoltan had never intended to tell them they could go. Maybe they were sacrificial lambs to be thrown on the pyre of his ill-gotten gains.

Almost as though he was summoned, Zoltan suddenly appeared on the screen of Gergely's laptop. He was still in the large room of the house in Budapest, but he didn't seem anywhere near as calm and collected as he had before. Rivulets of sweat were pouring down from the old man's brow. Gergely had the momentary thought that it must be hot for him too—until he realized Zoltan was a continent away.

"I have bad news," Zoltan said severely.

Gergely felt a spark of dread deep in his stomach. "What is that?"

"An FBI squad, along with several outside operatives, have invaded the warehouse outside Philadelphia."

The spark instantly mushroomed into a flame of panic. "You mean..."

"Yes, where we took the President. They have found him. We were able to watch the entire scenario through the video surveillance cameras we had placed inside."

If the President had been found... "What does that mean for our plans?" Gergely asked, though what he really wanted to ask was: "How are you going to extract me?"

"I don't know yet. I haven't decided."

Gergely swallowed deeply. It was just a matter of time.

"We have one factor on our side. The American government will need to confirm that the President is in fact the real one. That may take hours for them to process results. By that time, it will be too late for them."

Gergely did not see how it would take them hours. They must have identification software, or whatever, that could accomplish that purpose in mere minutes.

"What do you think I should do?" he said, trying to keep his voice from rising like a little girl's. "Maybe we should sneak out of here during the confusion."

"No!" Zoltan thundered. "Then they would find out that much sooner."

"But... you can't expect us to just sit here. We're sitting ducks now."

Zoltan gave him a long, hard stare that Gergely realized he must have been planning from the very start. Zoltan knew they would never get out.

"You cannot leave even if you wanted to. The White House is filled with Secret Service men who would stop you."

"So, we must just stay put?"

"Keep on buying us time," Zoltan said with a flinty voice. "Really, Gergely, you have no other choice."

CHAPTER 32

WITH NEW CLOTHES on, wrinkled from the backpack, Fredric walked into the kitchen. There were two bar stools lined up in the kitchen with the promised burger and drinks.

He pretended to take a sip out of the can of Heineken placed before him. Why did she think a German would like such a weak beer? "So, how long have you been with the FBI?" he asked.

"Four years. Jason told me that you are from overseas, but he didn't tell me what country. Where are you from, somewhere in Europe, I guess?"

"That's how I detected your Croatian accent. I'm from Vienna, Austria. I have traveled extensively throughout Europe. I don't really want to talk about my employer, though. I actually think of myself as my own employer," he said as he took a bite from the sandwich.

"How did you end up working for the FBI?" he asked, switching the subject back on to her.

"Well, I graduated from a law school in Chicago and got accepted into a competitive program in the Justice Department. I worked really hard in law school to get top grades and the work and volunteer experience that I knew the Justice Department prizes for bringing in freshly minted attorneys. It all started there," she said.

Then she too switched gears. "Tell me more about how you

found the warehouse in Philly. For that matter, tell me what led you to here in the U.S. in the first place," she said while taking another sip of wine and leaning toward him.

"I followed a trail," he said circumspectly. "I work quietly but very effectively. I don't talk or share my strategies. The people who I work for know that I am the best for a reason."

They continued to eat and drink. Fredric noticed there was jazz music playing in the background. George Benson was too light for his tastes, but he was pleasant. "Your radio must be battery powered to still be working."

"Ahh, it's a satellite radio, and yes, it is operating from a battery. I guess it won't be playing for too much longer," she said while smiling.

They soon were nearing the end of their meal. The bottle of Heineken remained untouched, but he'd chowed down the burger. He really was hungry.

"You are really handsome, Fredric. Is this trip taking you away from anyone you love dearly back in Vienna?"

His antenna was raised and broadcasting. What was this all about? "No, sadly no. My job makes relationships hard. I haven't had a steady significant other, if you will, for about three years."

"That's sad," she said as she put her hand on his arm.

Just then Fredric's phone rang. He answered it.

"This is Jason. Where are you, Fredric?"

That one question confirmed Fredric's suspicions. He moved the mouthpiece of the phone away and quickly whispered to Natasha, "It's him."

Unexpectedly, she grabbed the phone from him. "Jason, it's me. Natasha. Traffic is horrible. We are on the way. But we will be late because it's like a parking lot. We will see you soon." she said with a chuckle." "Can't talk now," she said as he concluded the call and turned the phone off.

Fredric thought he'd heard Lim shouting something before the connection was cut off. "We should get going."

"You are right, we do need to go. But let's just finish our drinks first."

Fredric firmly said, "I said, let's get going."

He stood up, hand raised inside his jacket. Any funny moves and he'd be asking questions later.

They walked back downstairs, Fredric following once again. This time he had his gun out, parked behind his back in case she turned around. They soon stepped outside and returned to Natasha's SUV. She pushed open the button on her key fob and Fredric got in the passenger side.

"Before we go, I am going to call Attorney General Lim to make sure we are still on course to take you to him." She stood just outside the driver's side of the vehicle with the phone to her ear.

"Hey Jason, sorry for the delay, we had a little traffic snafu, but all is OK. We are back driving again. Are we still going to your office? Oh really? That's too bad. I know Fredric was looking forward to seeing you." She looked at Fredric with an exaggerated sad face.

"Okay, we will go there. I will let him know. Sorry to hear about the delay, but those things happen."

As she pulled out of the apartment complex, Natasha said excitedly, "Fredric, the Attorney General told me that he now wants you to go to the location of the President and wait for further directions. He said you can take me there."

"He must be joking. I know they went *somewhere*, but I don't know where that *somewhere* is. Your people should move now," Fredric said with a firm tone.

"How about you call Sam? I don't have Sam's number with me right now because of a problem with the address book on my Blackberry. I can get it by calling back to the field office, but things are frantic there right now. Can you call him?"

Fredric was feeling extremely tense, watching her hands carefully. A little backup at this moment seemed like a very good idea. "Okay, I can try." Fredric got out the phone from his backpack and dialed Sam's number. Natasha pulled the car over in front of a fire hydrant near a big hotel a couple blocks away.

"Sam it's Fredric. Where are you? I went to go see Lim and he sent me one of your colleagues to pick me up and take me to his office. But he now wants me to come to where you are."

There was a pause on the line. "Is that right?" Sam said cautiously.

"Yes. He sent an agent to pick me up and we are trying to find where you are," Fredric repeated.

There was another pause on the line. "Uh, Fredric, where are you now?"

"I am parked in front of a big eight-story hotel that is about a block wide. The sign says Omni. Oh, and I see a street sign. We are on Calvert Street."

"I know exactly where you are. I will send a guy up to meet you. We are only about a few minutes away. And, my friend," Sam said, "keep your friends close, if you know what I mean."

"I think I do," Fredric said dryly. Putting away the phone, he relayed the apparent message to Natasha.

"He said we need to wait a few minutes. He has to get authorization for anyone who gets near the President."

"Sounds good," she said.

To be sure, Sam called the Attorney General to verify what was happening before he swung into action.

"Sir, the BND agent Fredric called me and let me know you wanted me to take him here. I am sending up one of my guys to escort him back here, as you requested, after we make sure he isn't being followed or otherwise compromised."

"Whoa, whoa, whoa. I sent someone to meet Fredric at Farragut Square and take him back here to my office so we could strategize, but he never showed up. I don't know what he is doing, but I do know that the Srepska mole who worked in my office just talked to me minutes ago. If that is the case, I bet she is using Fredric to find out where the President is. Under no circumstances can you let Fredric get anywhere near your facility."

"I thought as much. Fredric was very cagey on the phone when I talked to him just now."

Lim said, "This woman betrayed me and now she is trying to kill the President. Have agents go surround them and take them into custody."

The call concluded. Sam made a round of calls. They dispatched three FBI units to go to the location and secure the scene.

"I just hope, Fredric," Sam said after he hung up, "that you aren't collateral damage."

CHAPTER 33

TWO UNMARKED FOUR-DOOR Chevrolet sedans showed up, one white and one black. The passenger doors on each car opened as the cars came to a screeching stop.

"On the ground," one of the two agents gripping guns drawn at Natasha and Fredric shouted.

"Out of the car, hands up, on the ground," the other agent yelled emphatically.

Fredric froze. *Didn't Sam tell these guys the score?* he thought as he looked at their badges and jackets. He calmly opened the car door. He didn't want these nitwits to make any mistakes. Both of his hands were raised as he stepped out of the car and spread out on the roof.

Natasha began screaming. "Let me speak to Attorney General Lim. I work for him. Please, I am a Department of Justice employee. Look at my ID. I have done nothing wrong. This is a big mistake. Let me call him."

"Shut up," one of the agents said indifferently.

Fredric didn't think he would get anywhere, but he gave it a try anyway. "Call Sam Davis. He's FBI, but he's working for the Attorney General. I am working with him. So give him a call, because this is a big mistake."

"And I work for the Pope," the same agent chuckled.

The agents frisked Fredric and Natasha before handcuffing them both.

The agents then put Natasha and Fredric into the back seats of separate cars. Fredric watched as they placed Natasha's cellphone in a plastic Ziploc bag. At least she was being taken out of the action, so that was good. He'd be able to fend for himself.

A black Chevrolet Suburban arrived with a red light flashing on the inside dashboard. The two agents went over to Natasha's SUV and began to take out Fredric's backpack and Natasha's bag and opened them and laid out the contents on the hood.

The first two cars then pulled away.

After a ten-minute drive that felt like an hour to Fredric, the vehicles pulled into the Justice Department Building underground parking garage. The guard stationed at the driveway remarked to the driver of the first SUV, "You got a suspect back there? We sure don't see people in custody being brought here very often. You sure you aren't supposed to go to the FBI Washington Field Office?" the jovial guard remarked to the driver.

"Yes, we were ordered to come here."

They pulled in the garage and pulled up near the elevator bank and parked. The agents' ID cards got them into the elevators, and then past the security desk upstairs, and onto the elevators to the top floor.

The two agents took Fredric to a large conference room on the top floor, decorated with a long line of portraits. Fredric noticed that some were black and white images, some were color but taken decades earlier, and some were more modern. He noticed one at the end that appeared to be Lim.

The agents directed Fredric to sit down. They stood behind him, waiting. *I'm glad they have all the time in the world, because I sure don't.*

At last, Lim walked in and shut the door behind him.

"Uncuff this man. Why is he in handcuffs to begin with? I

never said to treat him like a common criminal. Get the handcuffs off NOW!"

"Yes, sir. Standard procedure," one of the two agents said.

Lim pulled up a chair and sat across from Fredric. He turned to the agents. "You can be dismissed. I know you have a lot of work you should be doing." They nodded, looking none too happy about being yelled at, and filed out the door.

Lim then came over to Fredric and the two men shook hands. "It's good to see you once again."

Lim pulled up a chair across the table from Fredric.

"Right now, the Navy is dispatching aircraft carriers and warships toward Burma. By all reports, we will very soon neutralize their out-matched military. The news says that China is about to mobilize its armed forces, possibly to intervene in Burma. We don't know, but the President is opening up a huge can of worms for the country. The stock market is closed, but when it reopens, you know it will drop…and drop like a brick. You may be the only other person in this building who can help unravel this mess. Tell me, what would you do next?"

Fredric glanced around the room, making sure they were alone. "I think Natasha might prove helpful. The FBI took her into custody, and I know where she lives, so her place could be searched."

Lim replied, "I suspected as much. I had her brought here, in case you needed anything from her. She is being held down the hall."

Fredric was glad to hear that. This Jason Lim had his head on straight, after all. "Maybe she should be brought in now. Also, they seized her phone, and we could check her recent calls."

Lim tapped some digits on his cell and said brusquely, "Bring in the prisoner. Also, bring in the phone of hers that you confiscated."

The two men waited in the silence of the large room until they heard shouting down the hall. "You have no right! Let me go!"

The door was opened, and Natasha was shoved through first. She was writhing against the rigid hold of the FBI agent behind him. "Let me go!"

"Sit down!" A second agent came in and together they man-handled her into a chair.

She was about to scream at them again when she noticed the steely gaze her former boss had trained on her. "Natasha," he said shortly.

"Jason…" she said, but she couldn't find any words to add. It was obvious that he knew what she'd done.

"You have been brought here because you can help us unravel the mystery of why the financial system of the United States has collapsed."

"Never! I will never tell you a thing!"

So far Fredric has been silent. He was quite sure he could make her talk, but he wasn't in Germany, and there were plenty of investigators here to handle any rough business. Instead he said mildly, "So nice to see you again, Natasha. You were so kind to feed me, and I must say, the meal was delicious."

"You're welcome," she said sullenly, confused by his pleasant manner.

"I was wondering if you would do me another favor. A big one this time." He rose out of his chair and walked toward her idly, like he didn't have a care in the world. "Tell me, do you have ties to your old country? Hungary, isn't it?"

A flash of alarm sparked in her eyes. Although she instantly recovered, he knew she had made the connection.

"You see, I came from that country just yesterday. I set up a wiretap at an address, and you wouldn't believe what I overheard. Do you perhaps know a fellow named Zoltan?"

This time she flinched, and Fredric realized that she was afraid of the man. So his guess about the origin of the attack was cemented. Now he just had to find the missing link between Budapest and Philadelphia.

"Excuse me," he said to the first FBI agent. "Did you bring in her phone?"

"Yes, I have it right here." He withdrew a plastic bag containing a blue Samsung Galaxy s7. "I have already opened it to the recent calls. Here, you can have a look."

Fredric, using the cloth that the agent handed him, started to scroll down the list of calls. The area code 202 appeared the most often, and he assumed that was for Washington, DC, since she worked there until a very brief time ago. He saw some random numbers, but one area code caught his eye: 540. Buried among all of the other calls, he noticed that she had been calling it every two hours on the dot: 11:22, 1:22, 3:22... He checked backward, and the pattern held throughout the daylight hours of the past two days.

"Tell me," he asked the agent, "where is the 301 area code?"

"Oh, that's Maryland, western Maryland."

"Is that far from here?"

"Well, it could be, but the area code starts just northwest of the city. It could be as close as five miles from here."

That seemed like an ideal location for an outfit like Srepska. Far enough away to stay out of sight, but close enough for someone to run into town in an emergency.

"Do you mind," he said, watching Natasha squirm, "finding out the closest cell tower for this number?"

CHAPTER 34

AFTER LARS HAD dropped Fredric off earlier, he didn't park. Instead, Lars zigzagged in and out of traffic that was stopped, or moving like molasses, on K Street. He drove several blocks, then looked at his phone again. *The spot I circled on the map is not here,* he thought. *I think I drove by it earlier.* He put his phone back in his pocket as he drove to a circular park he had passed. He then looked at his phone. *Why did I misread this map earlier? I now see where the dot is and it wasn't either place I thought it was.*

He drove back around to a street without much traffic and parked his motorcycle on the sidewalk. He saw a sign for Farragut Square ahead. *Maybe the map is going to lead me to a spot they use to make exchanges. Not sure what they would be exchanging, though. These people are very high-tech. Maybe it is a meeting spot instead.*

After Lars crossed the street and entered the park, he noticed a black SUV parked at the head of a block. It looked like the SUVs at the Pennsylvania warehouse. The driver, an older man with cross-cropped hair in a white shirt, was on a phone. It seemed as if he were emphatically making a point in a conversion.

Lars kept walking and then reached the corner of 17th Street and I Street. *This is the cash economy at its finest,* he thought as he saw a man selling t-shirts from a shopping cart near a hot dog stand, along with several other people with carts or bags waiting for a sale.

Lars looked down at his map. *This is the spot.* He noticed a sidewalk vendor who was selling fruit along Farragut Square. The vendor was wearing an unusual shade of gray jeans, with a ragged-looking Chicago Bears sweatshirt.

Lars joined a short line. "I will take a small container of chopped pineapple," he told the vendor.

The short twenty-something vendor waved a bug away and reached under the table to gather the fruit. The man handed it to him with a wide grin.

Lars kept looking around as he pondered what the dot on the map could refer to.

He ate the fruit as he walked back to his bike. *So, what good did that do me?* Something wasn't adding up, but whatever he'd done wrong, he wasn't going to find Srepska by eating pineapple chunks.

When he finished, he started up his motorbike. The traffic lights ahead were out. As he passed a police officer directing traffic, he glanced toward where he had just purchased his fruit. He noticed the fruit stand was still there, but the vendor was no longer standing behind it.

Then he heard a sudden loud rush of air. He turned around and saw his rear tire had gone flat. He then heard a bullet whiz by his head. He quickly threw himself off the motorcycle and landed on the nearby sidewalk, his fall cushioned by his thick cycling jacket and leather gloves. *I didn't hear a gunshot. But then again, the traffic is so noisy and everyone is honking their horn.*

Across the street, he saw the person who had sold him fruit was walking with his hand in his jacket. *That's a gun,* he thought. *The fruit stand must have been the spot on the map.* He slowly got up, as a small crowd began to congregate around him. Several people were asking "Are you okay? Can we help you?" One of the younger men, sporting a goatee and wearing a sports jacket and dress shoes, walked out into the street and picked up the motorcycle that was lying on the pavement, having crashed into the curb, and lifted it up off the street and activated the kickstand.

Conscious of the gunman stalking him, Lars burst to his feet. "I'm fine. Thanks for getting my bike. Can you bring it over here?"

"Yeah, man, the tire's blown. I guess you will have to walk it back home."

The person rolled the motorcycle over. It was noticeably slanted because of the blown-out back tire, which sagged to the side as the wheel spun around. A trio of busses passed on the street and stopped in the heavy traffic in front of him. He glanced in the gaps between them and did not see the fruit vendor. The sidewalk was blocked by the bus. He quickly walked the bike to a nearby parking meter. Keeping a watchful eye out constantly, he keyed in the lock password and inserted the chain through the front spokes. He geared the chain as tight as it would go, and slipped in the male end of the lock. He quickly opened the storage container on the back of the motorcycle and grabbed several items. He then left his motorcycle there, as he walked rapidly down the block. Still the busses hadn't moved. Still no shooter.

He turned down a side road off K Street. The office buildings he passed didn't offer much protection, but he saw a parking garage up ahead on the right. He could duck in there if needed. He weaved casually among the dozens of people on the sidewalk. *As long as I stay in these crowds, I have some protection,* he thought.

He gave a glance over his shoulder. The same man was behind him, trying to cross the street, but traffic began moving. They made eye contact, at least through the sunglasses that Lars was wearing. *I need to keep changing direction.*

He ran-walked down to the next block—I Street—and turned the corner. More office buildings. He noted a low wall topped with a flower bed, possible cover. Then on his right he spotted an alley. He looked down it and saw that it was really just a service drive-way. That would be just fine.

He hurried down the narrow lane and crouched behind a dumpster. He waited for a minute. No one came along. His quick turn onto I Street and then the next quick turn must have caused his stalker to lose sight of him. He could increase his odds even more, now that he had a moment to spare. He reached into his backpack and unzipped his black leather jacket. He folded it as tightly as possible. He took out a green fleece jacket from his backpack and put it on. The leather jacket went into the backpack.

Looking as much like an office drone as he could, he sauntered back onto the street. He walked behind a group of people heading back north. They looked like tourists, and they were chatting excitedly about the White House.

Lars spotted a park bench back in Farragut Square. *They won't expect me to be just sitting around. They expect me to be running for the hills.* He wanted to find out if he could spot any other member of their operation.

The traffic was still gridlocked. A drugstore on the corner had a "cash only" sign on it, as did the coffee shop next door. The screen on the ATM of a nearby bank was blank. He turned on his satellite radio and turned to a news channel. He learned that a company handling more than $5 trillion a day in foreign exchange transactions had temporarily ceased operations because of a system failure. A clearinghouse for nearly $2 trillion a day in domestic funds transfers also stopped operations because of problems with their normal computers as well as the backups.

Just then he saw the guy who had tried to shoot him coming back up 18th Street. The guy was trying to look inconspicuous as he searched in every direction.

Lars froze. Sitting there no longer seemed like such a good idea. The fruit stand guy could recognize him, and then he would be a sitting duck.

Lars saw a bus lumber by. He got up and dashed into the gap behind it. The car following it honked its horn and screeched its brakes to stop. *Great*, he thought, *why not make a public announcement?* He finished crossing the street and dashed toward an office building next to the coffee shop. He pulled on the door, and it opened.

The security guard had stepped away from the reception desk, he saw as he calmly walked to the stairwell. He climbed the stairs and got off on the second floor. Numerous offices lined the hallway. He tried the first door, which had a sign that it was an accountant's office.

The door was locked.

The next door, for an attorney, was also locked.

He headed for the door at the far end of the hallway. *It probably lines up with the bench where I was sitting outside.* Naturally, the door was locked.

Lars was getting tired of all the security-conscious drones. He swung his backpack around. Opening it, he pulled out a small battery-powered device and fit it into the lock. He gripped it several times in a pumping motion, and the lock cylinder turned.

He walked in and noticed an alarm panel near the door. But the LCD panel was dead…it had no power, so it couldn't ring an alarm.

He locked the door and walked over to the window. There was no sign of the man who had been following him. He still needed answers, and it occurred to him that maybe the guy at the fruit stand could supply them.

He walked back to the door, turned the deadbolt lock to unlock it, and opened the door a couple inches. He got his handgun out and held it down to his side. Within a minute, he heard the stairwell door opening down the hall. He saw the same guy's head poke into the hall before turning toward him. "Down here," he said at an elevated voice that wasn't quite a shout.

He went back in the office, keeping the door ajar. He rapidly walked to the coat closet and stepped inside. He kept the door far enough ajar that he could see when the assassin walked in.

The front door creaked open just a bit. *Too bad I cannot see the door. But I know someone is entering.* As he peeked through the crack of the door, he saw the man with blue jeans walk in silently while revolving a Beretta APX in front of him. Lars's heart began racing even faster. *This is a gift on a silver platter,* he thought. *I cannot wait to see what is in his pockets and get his phone.*

When the man had passed him, Lars flung open the closet door and sprinted toward him. "Drop the gun! Now!"

Instead the man swung around with incredible speed and lashed out with his leg. Lars dodged the thrust to his face. He stepped inside and lashed out with his pistol, slapping the man full across the cheek. Then he swiftly raised his right leg and struck the man's right knee. His enemy howled with pain and began swearing.

Lars didn't lose his advantage. He whipped around the pistol again, smashing it into the man's temple, hoping to knock him out. His assailant stumbled sideways, and this time Lars kicked the Beretta out of his hands. With his left hand, he launched a roundhouse that smacked him in the other temple.

Like a sack the man collapsed to the floor.

Lars shouted as the man writhed in pain, "You loser! You caused me to crash my cycle. You really messed up the plans for my day, did you know that?"

The man started to come to and his hand reached out for Lars's foot. Coolly, Lars shot him between the eyes. The explosion boomed in the silent space, but Lars doubted anyone was around to hear it. Cursing his luck—he just wanted to ask the guy a few questions—he dragged the man's body into the closet. He kicked the body angrily. "That's for my motorcycle."

Leaning down, Lars patted the man's pockets. He found a wallet that contained a driver's license with an address in Poolesville, Maryland. He took the ID out and put it into his pocket. Keying up his phone, he found out that Poolesville was a suburb just outside the city. *My trip to DC has suddenly become worthwhile,* Lars thought. *Now how am I going to get to this address?*

He walked out of the office, down the hallway, and back down the stairs. Crossing the lobby, he tried to call Fredric's number. He got a recording, *All circuits are busy. Please try your call again later.* He tried again once he was fully outside. Luckily, the phone began ringing.

"Fredric, this is Lars. Where are you?"

"I'm downtown at the Attorney General's office."

"Look, I've discovered an address that is worth checking out. The problem is, some good for nothing shot out the back tire on my bike. How about we meet up again?"

"Good idea," Fredric said. "I have not been idle myself. I was able to obtain the cellphone of a Srepska agent, and I came up with an address in Poolesville, Maryland. It's a funny name, like a town that has a lot of pools, but I think it is worth checking out."

Lars felt a cold rush roll through his body. "No way. The address I have is in Poolesville too."

"I think we're on to something."

"I think so too. Look, can you get a hold of a government car?"

"At this point, I think they would give me the key to the city. Yes, I'll ask them. Tell you what. I'm going to get one of those gigantic black vehicles everybody has been driving around."

Lars smiled, a tremendous relief after nearly being shot to death. "Pick me up at the corner of 19th and L streets," he said.

CHAPTER 35

PETER CAMPBELL, THE Chief of Staff, had been alerted almost as soon as President Evans was rescued. At first, he was completely confused. An FBI Special Agent informed him that Evans had been found in a warehouse outside of Philadelphia. Campbell protested, "How could that be possible? The President is downstairs in the Situation Room."

"I'll connect you with him."

In the interval while Campbell was waiting, the wheels in his head were already turning. He had thought the President was acting strangely ever since he returned from the Treasury Building. The proposed attack on Myanmar was monstrous. Sure, they could invade the backward country, but the idea came out of nowhere. The President had never talked about Myanmar. Plus, it didn't make any sense. The last place anyone would look for computer know-how was a country that went into self-imposed isolation for forty decades.

Any lingering doubts Campbell had were removed when the President came on the line. Campbell recognized his boss's voice immediately.

"But Mr. President, how…"

"Never mind the how," the President growled. "When I track down the people who did this, I'm going to make sure they sit in solitary for the rest of their sorry lives."

Campbell offered, "What do you want me to do?"

"I am being driven back to Washington as we speak. The Secret Service, not to mention the Joint Chiefs of Staff, think it is wise that I stay away from the White House until they clear it of these Srepska people."

"And that will happen when?"

"I believe they already have the operation under way. They just want to make sure the take-downs are done without any loss of lives, especially of our staff."

"So, I should just sit tight?"

"Yes," the President said. "Don't give them any hint that you know. But, of course, also don't allow them to give any further directives about Myanmar. Or any other subject, for that matter."

"I assume that we're already handling the Myanmar situation."

"Yes, the Navy has been ordered to return its ships to their base in Guam. The Chinese have been sent a preliminary message to disregard any further word about Myanmar."

"So, we're in the clear."

"Well, if you consider the United States being in total financial disarray 'the clear,' I suppose you're right."

Campbell coughed nervously. "Sorry, sir, I just meant as far as—"

"I'll be back in touch very shortly."

***

Gergely couldn't stand the pressure of waiting any longer. Several hours had passed since Zoltan's Skype. The real President had been found. It was just a matter of time before armed soldiers rapped on the door to the Situation Room. Then Gergely would be handcuffed and escorted off to a jail cell that he would occupy for the rest of his life.

"We can't just stay here," he told his companions. "They'll be coming for us sooner or later."

"You know what Zoltan said," said Andor, sitting to his right.

"I don't care what he said!" Gergely shouted. "He doesn't care about us. Haven't you figured that out yet?"

Yet neither of his companions answered. It was evident that they were more scared of Zoltan than anything the Americans might do. And he couldn't blame them for that. He didn't know, however, if he could sit in a jail cell for the rest of his life. American prisoners were animals. He had heard all about that. He wasn't strong. He wasn't even a very good criminal.

He bolted to his feet. "I say we should make a run for it."

His two companions looked at him like he was crazy. "How do you propose to do that?"

"We'll just walk out normally, like anyone would expect. As long as we stay out of sight—"

"It will never work. I, for one, do not have a death wish."

"Nor do I," Gergely said, wondering if he was right, after all. Again the idea of a life sentence in prison came to his mind. He couldn't do that. He would rather... yes, he would rather be shot, he would rather die.

"I am going," he told them. "I must take the chance."

His legs felt wooden as he crossed to the door, and his hands felt like ham hocks as he turned the knob. Maybe he should stay put. He was exposing himself to terrible risks.

Yet he continued out the door, not looking back. He glanced down the hallway and saw no one. He remembered that the elevator was—no, they would expect him to come up the elevator. He would find a staircase... There, just beyond the elevators was a red-lit exit sign. For the stairs.

He walked down the hall, not obeying the urge to run as far as he could to hide out of sight. He reached a metal door with a pane of glass. Opening it, he found himself inside an industrial staircase, like one found in any office building in the world. Hurriedly ascending the metal-rimmed steps, he climbed to a landing and then reversed course up to the next floor.

Peeking out another window, he saw a hallway that looked like the one they had used when they came in. He couldn't see left or right, so he cautiously started to open the door. No, be bold, he told himself, the President would march right down the hall like he owned the place.

He swung the door open and stepped out into the open. He nearly gasped when he saw a fully armed soldier in camouflage some ways down the corridor. The way he would have to pass to leave the building. Gulping, he started forward. He would have to bluff his way out.

As he passed the soldier, he gave a half salute, like he imagined the President would do with a member of the world's finest army. He almost said, "Carry on," but he worried that his voice could give away his slight accent.

He had walked on past when he heard a loud voice: "Excuse me! Stop and identify yourself!"

Ice ran through his veins as he turned around. It was the soldier, with his rifle held level. "Identify myself?" he said, trying to force a laugh. "Don't you know who I am? I am the President, your commander-in-chief."

He wheeled back around again and started walking.

"I said stop!" the soldier warned. "If you do not stop, I will not be responsible for what happens!"

Gergely kept walking, fast, despite the fear that was overtaking his every limb. At any second he expected gunfire to open up.

Finally, he could stand the tension no longer. He could see the door where he had entered, what seemed like a lifetime ago. He broke into a full-out run. If he could just get outside—

A single shot exploded in the hallway. Gergely felt a gigantic hole ripped into his back. In the same second a crater erupted in his chest. Where his heart was. Seeing the splash of blood, spurting from his own body, he had the fleeting thought that he couldn't live with his heart like that...

Until he collapsed and knew no more.

CHAPTER 36

"SCOUTING OUT A remote location is going to be risky for us. But it is the address we both have. Let's see what we will find," Fredric told Lars. "Hopefully, this is their American center of operations."

Lars looked out at other traffic on the interstate from the passenger seat. "It's important that we get in and get out quickly," he said.

Soon, the duo were driving across a one-lane bridge on a country road that was so narrow that one of the locals pulled as far as to the right on the road as possible when she approached them.

"You see?" Fredric cried. "When you have a big car, people get out of your way."

Lars gave him a hard look from across the seat. "You're a tough guy, aren't you? Making jokes when we're liable to get our heads blown off."

On the radio, they heard an all-news channel from Wilmington, Delaware. "The electric companies are at a loss to explain why many customers in the Midwest and Eastern states do not have power, other than that there are massive system failures at the key power relay stations and power generation plants. Utility officials are scrambling to make timely repairs."

Fredric thought about what he had heard back in Jason Lim's office. Stocks overseas were falling fast, and stock exchanges in the United States had closed early due to "circuit breakers" that shut the brokerages down when they fell greater than a certain percentage in a short time frame. "The U.S. Treasury is probably not the safest place for risk-averse investors," Lim had remarked.

"This is it," Lars announced, looking at the mailbox after they rounded a bend. "Boy, I wonder how long the driveway behind the gate is."

"Let's drive down a ways," Fredric told him. He strained to peer through the line of trees along the county road. "We cannot see anything from here."

"Down this road could be a farmer sitting on his front porch watching the sunset. Or there could be a lethal well-trained small army," Lars remarked.

"Shall we park and try to enter the property by jumping over the fence?" Fredric said. *This type of operation is new ground for me,* he thought as he started to feel flickers of apprehension.

"Let's park in the little pull-off area we just passed a quarter mile away, in the more wooded area we drove through," Lars suggested. "I bet that hunters park there. Let's go find a hunting trail that will probably start near there that we can use as a jumping-off point."

Fredric turned around, executing a quick turn with the huge vehicle, and found the turnoff that Lars had pointed out. They soon were walking on a trail. Fredric used his compass to get their bearings in case they had to escape quickly. The woods grew thicker, and they began pushing back branches while trying to softly walk on the leaves that covered the ground.

This is sure thick underbrush, Fredric thought. *There's no drought around here for sure. At least these gloves are super-sturdy,* he thought as he repositioned the Velcro on his glove tightly against his sweater.

"This must be the property," Lars said soon as they reached a rusty fence about half of his height with a single strand of barbed wire on top.

"If this is the place we are after, there are going to be motion detectors and sensors all around here. Or else trained attack dogs."

Lars knew from his law enforcement training that dogs could be waiting quietly for them to come through and then suddenly attack. He thought of how those might be more likely to be used as the first line of defense than motion detectors, given the likelihood that they would be triggered by deer and other wildlife regularly.

They kept walking, stopping every couple minutes to listen for footsteps. Fredric began to feel danger when all he heard was an eerie silence. He thought back to his time in the military and how everything went quiet before approaching an ambush. He wondered if he would be as lucky as he was one time when a sharp-eyed and fast-fingered buddy neutralized the Taliban sniper before he or his team were injured.

"Stop. Up there—an infrared camera," Fredric whispered. "It is fixed in position, so there are probably others."

"We haven't triggered it yet, but we will if we keep going," Lars responded. "The good news is, we're on the right path."

Lars threw his backpack down.

"What are you doing," Fredric asked, perplexed.

He pulled out his laptop computer and pushed a card into the USB port on the side and turned it on.

"I can bet you, there are no cables out here. The cameras are connected to the monitoring unit wirelessly. We are going to scan and find the frequency these cameras are using to transmit their feed. Then we are going to mess with it."

"Did you make that yourself?" Fredric asked, having never seen anything like it before.

Lars said, "I'm proud of this device. I built it myself, using a combination of instructions available over the internet, electronic components, and some experimentation. You'll see, it really works."

After several minutes, Lars pulled out a small black box that had wires on top and turned two knobs as LEDs lit. "This will mess with the transmissions. Their security system is bound to have anti-jamming technology, but they won't know whether what we are doing is a deliberate attempt to jam or a malfunction or other interference.

The main thing is, they won't be able to see us as long as this is on." Lars stuck the device in the pocket of his coat.

We are walking into a virtual minefield, Fredric thought. *We need to be looking up every tree.*

After they went a little farther, they heard barking. *This isn't as easy to get around. Gunfire would be a dead give-away that we are here. Still, we need to do something quickly.*

Fredric pulled out his gun. Mounting the silencer, he waited until two German shepherds swarmed into view. Two soft *pffts!* put them down.

Lars felt stunned and his jaw dropped as the barking stopped.

"Are you okay," Fredric asked as he saw the look of horror on Lars's face. *I can't believe this. He didn't seem shaken up after he killed that guy in Philadelphia.* "I'm sorry. I like dogs myself."

Lars had already recovered. "It's fine. I've just never had to do that before."

They soon reached the edge of the tree line and saw a gravel road. Fredric thought that that there were probably sensors near the gate but not likely here. "I think we can follow the road a bit, but let's stay close to the tree line." *There isn't much tree cover to hide us if suddenly we hear a car, but it will be the best we can do.*

"You smell that?" Lars asked within a couple moments.

"No. What is it?"

"Cigarette smoke. I don't smell it now, but I smelled a whiff."

Fredric clutched his gun more tightly. *They are coming to check on the camera, I suspect. They may not have heard the dogs barking, depending on where the guards are stationed or if they did, they might have thought it was a deer.*

"This sure looks like a temporary setup," Lars noted quietly. "It is like they added some high-tech equipment to a house they rented. If they were going to be here longer, they would have a smarter fence. We would have seen a small white dome-shaped device that would have been the ground-based radar system."

"Let's not walk together up there," Fredric said abruptly. "We should stay in eye contact of each other but move separately."

"Fine. How about you go first, and signal with your hands if you need to tell me something? And keep your eye out for more cameras." Lars turned the knob on his jammer off and put it back in his backpack.

Within a couple minutes, as they were rounding a bend, Fredric bolted into the woods. Lars's eyes jumped to a downed tree.

Suddenly, Lars saw what was coming his way. A man was holding a small black tube up to his eye.

"Stop, who are you?" the man shouted. *The guy has a gun too,* Lars realized. *The guy may think I am a hunter. But he is suspicious because the camera is jammed.*

Lars started staggering and laughing. "Someone who wants a couple more cold ones! Ben, you got the beers?"

"Stop, who are you?"

"Why you acting all weird, Ben? What took you so long? And where did this road come from?" Lars said as he kicked the ground and laughed again.

The man aimed his gun at Lars as he studied his every move. *This ruse is going to work, but only for a few more seconds,* Lars thought. *He won't shoot me if he thinks I am a lost hunter because he will think my friend will come looking for me or call the police.*

Just then Fredric sprinted from out of the tree line. With his right fist cocked, he punched with lethal force into the base of the man's skull just above the fold of the neck. Fredric was probably at least a hundred pounds heavier than the man, and he went down like a stone.

"Is that what you do?" Fredric asked. "Act drunk?"

"It worked, didn't it?" Lars said. "Come on, we better get moving in case this guy has some friends."

CHAPTER 37

FREDRIC DRAGGED THE man's body into the trees. "Let's take the battery out of his phone and radio," Lars whispered as he reached into his pockets.

Meanwhile, Fredric felt a momentary sense of calm as he looked through the night scope and didn't see any others. *I have spent more time lately using one of these in training exercises than on real assignments,* he thought.

"Let's keep moving," Fredric said. They walked for another few minutes as they followed the road around a curve and realized a house was a short distance in front of them.

"What is our plan from here?" Lars asked.

"Do we want to take it ourselves or get support?" Fredric asked as he began to calculate the odds. They would surely be outnumbered and they didn't know the layout of the house.

"Whatever we do, we need to move quickly. They are probably getting suspicious by now if the guy they sent to check on the camera didn't come back."

"We need to create a distraction of some sort to lure them out."

"That's a possibility. But there's only two of us, so let's figure how to make the most of that. First, though, we need to figure what do we want to do," Fredric asked. "In that house is gathered a bunch of Srepska agents. They might have some men who know their way around a weapon, but they probably figured that the dogs and motion sensors would take care of their problems," Fredric said.

Lars nodded in agreement. He surveyed the large house from end to end. It was a Georgian mansion built of brick with stone trim for the windows and doors. "We didn't come all this way to find their location and then turn around," he said. "I'll be honest with you. We probably have far more expert training and experience with raids like this than they do in defending against one. Plus, if just you and me go in and do this, we don't have to worry about the authorities questioning why we did what we did or get in the way. You remember back in Philly, they were going to keep us out of the operation entirely."

"There is just one car there," Fredric pointed out. "Unless they are hiding them, which I doubt."

"You are right," Lars said. "Let's do it. You go first, I will cover you. But we have to be prepared for a fight."

"I am always prepared," Fredric said, looking intently at the house.

Lars was stopped short again. Then he swatted Fredric on the shoulder and said, "I'm sure you are."

The two of them sidled to their right, until they were facing one end of the large structure. Even from across the lawn they could see that there was no activity going on inside the rooms they were facing. "Do you see any motion sensors on the house?" Fredric asked quietly.

They both surveyed the brick front, but they couldn't spy anything.

"It's possible they have some micro device," Lars said, "but I don't see why they would. I think they counted on their outer defenses detecting any intruders."

"I agree," Fredric said, still assessing the situation.

"So, you want to make a break for it?" Lars asked.

Fredric nodded. "The spoils belong to the bold."

Staying low on his feet, he scrambled across the expanse of lawn toward a side door waiting for them. The distance wasn't far, and he covered the distance in a few seconds. Rising to his full height, he stood with his body pressed against the bricks. For several long seconds, he waited for any signs of an alarm going off inside the house.

Finally satisfied, he signaled for Lars to join him. The American scuttled across the green lawn in a similar crab-like fashion, his head darting both left and right. He ended up standing next to Fredric, a mere foot from a window flanking the door. Stealthily, he leaned his head forward until he could see the room inside.

"It's empty," he whispered.

Fredric thought as much, but to make sure, he crossed the doorway and carefully leaned out across the window on the far side. That too was vacant. From the clothes hanging on the furniture, it looked like it had been abandoned for some time.

"Let's go in," he hissed as he returned to Lars.

They exhibited the same professional caution as they searched all sides of the door for any alarm wires. It seemed that no one had rigged anything.

"If they have a wireless system, we cannot help that," he said in Lars's ear, and the American shrugged in agreement.

Both of them took out their weapons and held them ready up by their heads. Fredric slowly opened the screen door. Midway through, a creak of the hinge momentarily startled him. *We cannot have any more missteps like that to let them know we are coming,* he thought. Keeping the screen door opened only that far, he turned the large brass knob of the door. The door was unlocked.

Opening it ever so slowly, he peered through the crack until he could see a hallway with a high ceiling. The place looked dingy, like it hadn't been painted in years. He turned around enough to see that Lars was holding the screen door. He waved his gun slightly to signal that he was going in.

As he stepped inside the house, he could feel that Lars was following right behind. He waited until they could march forward side by side. As he passed the door to the room on the right, he already knew it was empty, but he scanned every foot of it with his gun set to fire. Simultaneously, Lars checked the room on his side.

They kept advancing, and Fredric kept one eye on the wide floorboard under his feet. They were old, and that meant they might creak as well. Yet they were well fitted, and they approached the other end of the hall without making a sound.

As the door opening came closer, Fredric slid in front of Lars, turning sideways to present a slimmer profile to anyone in the next room. Keeping inside the left door frame as much as possible, he edged up to the opening. Now he could hear humming. He recognized it from the house in Philadelphia—the hum of computer servers.

They were getting close.

Fredric turned to Lars and cupped his ear, rising his eyebrows in a question. After a moment, Lars nodded to indicate that he heard the noise too. Fredric used his non-gun hand to slant out to the right. He pointed at Lars and slanted his hand out to his left. When they burst through the doorway, they would take positions on either side. Lars wagged his gun to the left to show he understood.

Fredric exaggerated the crouch he adopted, to show Lars he was ready to spring. Then he shot through the door, the barrel of his gun ready for anything. Behind him he felt the swish of Lars barreling to the left.

In a flash, he took in a half dozen people sitting at a dining room table, their faces lit by laptop screens. "Everybody, freeze!" he shouted.

Storming forward, he kept his gun trained, ready to fire if anyone made the slightest motion.

"Everybody, hands up in the air!" Lars shouted, racing right beside him. "I said, hands up! Now! Up in the air!"

"Please don't shoot," said one of them, a lanky blond nerd. "I'll do what you say."

Fredric spotted movement in the far doorway and he fired. A man shouted out in agony and twisted around at the bullet's impact. Fredric rushed forward. Crossing through the opening, he lashed out with his shoe and kicked the gunman's AK-47 out of his hand. The sub-machine gun clattered against the nearest wall.

"You, get up on your feet," Fredric said, his voice a deadly growl.

Yet the man only writhed on the floor, holding his stomach. Fredric had fired center mass, and he could tell from the wound's entry site that the man would die a slow, painful death. In another moment, Fredric slashed him across the temple and knocked him out. Put him out of his misery, was more like it.

He quickly retreated back into the doorway, looking in all directions for the sign of any other guards.

In the meantime, Lars had the six techies covered. Going from one to the next, he bound their hands together with plastic cuffs, then forced their bound arms behind their chair backs and cuffed them to the chair. "Nobody makes one peep, do you hear me?" he kept threatening.

They were obviously trained hackers, and nothing else, because they all looked terrified. The blond one who had spoken up before pleaded as Lars cuffed him. "Please don't hurt me." As Lars yanked his arms behind the chair, the room filled with the smell of urine being spilled.

Fredric heard footsteps in the distance, sounding like they were coming down from overhead. He trained the barrel on the majestic staircase that went up to the second floor. When he saw the first sign of a leg coming around the banister, he shouted:

"There is a whole team outside. Drop your gun now or we take you down!"

He saw a long dark object being thrown and then an AK-47 crashed against a wall and stuttered down the wide stairs. Fredric darted forward and grabbed it. Holstering his handgun, he held the weapon out in a firing stance.

"Come out where I can see you! Walk slowly or I'll shoot!"

A tall, heavyset man appeared on the landing. Taking each step carefully, his hands held high, he descended the stairs. His eyes widened at the sight of his countryman lying sprawled on the floor, blood forming a pool around his waist. When he reached the bottom, Fredric quickly patted him from behind for other weapons.

"All right," he said, backing out of reach, "go through the door and join your friends."

Fredric followed him in, keeping his weapon trained on everyone in the room. Lars pointed for the newcomer to take another chair.

"Why are you shaking?" Lars asked.

The man looked down sheepishly. "I know who you both are. Please, I don't want any trouble. I don't want to die."

Lars turned to Fredric. "I guess there are no Purple Hearts in this crowd."

Fredric smiled tightly, too wound up to enjoy the wisecrack. "I'll go search the rest of the house. I don't think there are any more, but better safe than sorry."

"I'll call for the cavalry," Lars said as he finished cuffing the last of them. When he saw that Fredric didn't understand, he added, "I'll call the FBI. They'll need their computer forensic guys to untangle this mess."

As Fredric set off to search the rest of the mansion, Lars called the number Sam had given him. He reported the location and requested a large enough contingent to process eight individuals. "At least so far," he said at the end. "We think we have all of them."

Then he hung up and turned his attention to the techies. He decided to pick on the blond guy. He was the chicken of the bunch, and he'd be the likeliest to spill his guts.

"We will let you walk if you help us," Lars promised, knowing he'd do no such thing. "Let's start with this question. How did VISA and MasterCard and all the financial networks get brought down?" he asked.

"Easy," the man replied. "The people I work for found the locations of dedicated servers and then tracked down entry points into these networks."

As he continued to talk, Lars could keep track of most of what he was saying. Cloud networking became the thing that everyone had to do a few years ago. The whole concept was sold in the name of business continuity to be prepared for a disaster. Businesses stored all their programs, their systems, their information on virtual servers now. This meant that these financial and investment companies and their service providers outsourced all their systems to several big companies that operated server farms. Srepska found and wormed their way into them.

"And then what," Fredric asked.

"They launched an attack on the backbones for the two main payment cards in the U.S., VISA and MasterCard." *Of course*, Lars thought. *The utilities that connect cards, merchants, ATMs, and banks and allow you to swipe your card. The merchant knows the card is good for the transaction, and you to walk out the door with whatever you wanted to buy. That's why I couldn't use my MasterCard, but people could use VISA back when I was getting my smoothie before starting this operation.*

"So what did you do once you went into these servers or systems or whatever it was?" Lars asked.

"We delivered malware literally bit by bit, in small increments, into the systems. A single line of code wasn't that suspicious. But lots of small pieces were pieced together. It caused records and files to get contaminated in a way that drove the computer systems crazy trying to figure out what was happening. The previous data was deleted, accounts were mismatched. Think of a big puzzle where someone came through and took out a handful of pieces and replaced them with pieces from completely different puzzles."

Good luck figuring that out, Lars thought.

"Anything else you want to add?" Lars added. *The breadth of the attack would require some fairly sophisticated planning. I bet there were separate but coordinated attacks on several completely independent organizations and their computer systems. This guy probably does not know it all.*

"A DDOS," the man said sheepishly. Srepska used many computers to coordinate distributed denial of service attacks on the websites of these companies. They basically overwhelmed the computers with junk web traffic and overworked them until they shut down

"Wait a second," Lars told the man as Fredric reappeared.

He and Fredric came together and huddled. "This guy is really a wimp. He's been telling me everything," Lars said. "What do you think the underlying motive of Srepska is here?" Lars asked.

"Remember what I told you, the conversations I heard over in Budapest, they are trying to crash the U.S. economy so that investments they made will net them huge sums of money. They placed millions of dollars of stock trades and purchases of hard assets that could net billions if the plan worked as it was envisioned," Fredric said.

"Ahh, yes. And, chances are, all the investment bets were made overseas, and likely outside the stock markets. Anytime there is turmoil in the world, certain types of assets, such as gold, rise in value and rise fast," Lars noted. He began thinking. *One of the biggest data breaches in recent history was caused by a large multinational company's heating and air conditioning contractor being an easy entry point into the large company's network where the thieves were able to operate undetected. Data security systems are like an impenetrable fortress around a small town, but if you can find a creek that isn't well secured during a low-water point and you can get under the wall, you can do whatever you want because the security administrators are so focused on keeping the bad guys from getting through the walls that they don't dedicate anywhere near the same resources to monitoring what is happening inside.*

"What do you propose we do?" Fredric asked.

Just then the silence was pierced by rapidly approaching sirens. Lars and Fredric looked at each other.

"I'd say it's time to skedaddle, brother. I trust that Sam guy, but I wouldn't trust the rest of the government as far as I can throw them."

Fredric did smile for real this time. "Yes, I think that even a BND agent would spend a long time answering questions about shooting a man on American soil."

Much more quickly than they had entered the house, they hurried back out the side door. They were safely into the cover of the woods before they saw the first of the black SUV's hurtling up the driveway.

CHAPTER 38

A PRESS CONFERENCE was hastily scheduled at the U.S. Department of Justice. Attorney General Jason Lim had a special announcement.

Lim walked in and stood at the podium. On each side of him were men and women in dark suits with sober faces. Some had firearms on their waist and a badge, others not. Clearly, these people were a mix of law enforcement officials and prosecutors.

"I have shocking news. The person who has been issuing statements from the White House claiming to be the president has been an imposter. President Evans was kidnapped by the sophisticated international gang that has compromised the U.S. financial system and nearly started a deadly war."

After a long pause, he continued. "Serious criminal activities have taken place before within a few months of a presidential transition, but what has happened here raises the threshold for what criminal minds may try to accomplish. Thanks to the dedicated work of law enforcement, we have identified the operatives of this outfit in the United States and are able to bring them to justice. We rescued the rightful president, and he is here with us today."

In walked the President of the United States—the real one. He approached the podium. He was wearing blue jeans and a sports jacket. Consistent with his unscripted, somewhat unconventional personality, he spoke impromptu for ten minutes about the ordeal.

"It is a testament to the American people and our government that we safely and peacefully averted a crisis that could have placed our nation in serious jeopardy. When I practiced medicine, I often counselled my patients that a stitch in time saves nine. In other words, catch a problem early and you can avoid potentially irreversible harm. Well, that same concept and advice applies here too."

Fredric and Lars had a beer together at the Prospect bar in Washington. Fredric had scheduled an 11:54 flight back to Germany. It would cost a fortune, but Fredric figured the BND owed him a little something. Lars was telling him that he was looking forward to going for a long run around the Rose Bowl. It had been several days since he last visited his favorite workout spot.

"You know, I wonder what impact taking down the biggest terrorism in history will have on my business."

"They will be lining up for your services," Fredric said, laughing. "I know I would hire you in a second."

Lars smiled, but he was serious as he said, "Make sure you put in a good word with your boss."

They were watching a TV, and the news commentators were certain that in the weeks ahead, the full power of the United States and its Justice Department would ensure that the Srepska operatives caught could be expected to spend the rest of their natural lives in a high-security federal prison. Federal officials were quick to boast that they had brought down this crime syndicate. After all, they had caught several men in a warehouse in Pennsylvania and killed the presumable ringleader who was posting as President.

"Did they ever say what they're going to do about Srepska headquarters in Hungary?" Fredric asked Lars.

"Who knows? That's above my pay grade."

"You would think, with all the agreements the United States has in Europe," Fredric said, then paused. "Of course, for all we know, that house in Budapest has been cleared out for hours by now. That's the rotten part of crime these days. You pack up some computers in a truck, and it's on to the next hack."

"And then they'll have to bring us in again to save the day."

Lars raised his hand, and this time Fredric high-fived him right away. "Yes, German efficiency and American boldness. I would say that's a winning combination."